With My Last Breath

The Bloodstone Saga

By Courtney Cole

Dedication

To my Grandma Helen.
She is no longer here to see this,
but I know that she knows.

CONTENTS

CHAPTER ONE

I was floating in a dark place, a place where I was all alone. The blackness was consuming. It filled me up and I drifted on it as it ebbed and flowed peacefully all around me, the warmth calming me with soothing fluidity. Until cackling, bitter laughter abruptly pulled me from the lovely darkness, reminding me of what had caused me to lose consciousness in the first place.

Moros.

The sound of the ancient woman snapped me back to reality as quick as a bolt of lightning. A brief image of my soul mate, Cadmus, with Moros' deadly sister Thanatos ricocheted through my mind, accompanied by an ever-widening ripple of panic and a stuttering heart beat. He was in danger.

I emerged from my imaginary tranquil pool as my eyes popped open. Staring into Moros' faded eyes, I watched for a split second as crimson blood ran in rivulets from the corner of her eye and streaked down her wrinkled cheek, dripping onto her black cloak. I shuddered. Her eyes continually bled from all of the horror that she had seen, all of the pain that she had inflicted as an enforcer of the Fates throughout the millennia. It had turned her into a monster.

"What have you done?" I hissed as I sprang to my feet and shot out of my bedchambers like a rocket.

Cadmus was my only focus as I charged down the cascading marble staircase of Zeus' palace in a blinding streak of motion. We had just gone to hell and back as the Fates and their sisters, the Keres, had imprisoned all of the gods and goddesses of Olympus and the surrounding Spiritlands. They had entranced my husband, Cadmus, in the process and I had only just gotten him back. This couldn't be happening.

I barely noticed the banquet attendees who were laughing and sipping Olympian nectar and dancing carefree around the twinkling, lantern-adorned courtyard as I pushed through them to plunge into the sweetly scented dark night outside.

My mother, Aphrodite, froze in place when she saw me, apprehension immediately pooling in her eyes. She grabbed my father's arm and Ares turned toward me as well, his chiseled face instantly wary.

"Harmonia, what is it?" Aphrodite quickly asked, anxiety etched on her perfect face. She knew from simply looking at me that something was horribly wrong. She almost knew me better than I knew myself.

It was impossible to answer her because I couldn't even breathe as I scanned the perimeter of the crowd to locate the exact place where Cadmus had been standing just a few minutes earlier. His tall frame was gone.

He and Annen, an ancient Keres priest, had been there just two minutes ago. But now there was nothing, just the blackness of the Spiritlands night closing in on us as the stars twinkled overhead. I struggled to catch my breath as I frantically searched through the crowd.

Nothing.

But just as I started to turn away, I caught a glimpse of Olympus residents congregating in a circle on the edge of the courtyard, murmuring in panic. My stomach dropped like a lead weight and I innately knew that Cadmus was among them. I also knew that something was very, very wrong.

Placing one numb foot after the other, I woodenly approached and the crowd parted to allow me to pass. Stunned faces stared at me from the circle but I paid them no mind. My gaze was frozen on my soul mate.

Cadmus was lying on his back in the middle of the circle, completely still and quiet. The angles from his bronzed face caught the light of nearby lanterns and as always, his beauty was staggering. His hair was dark and shiny, his muscular body lithe and taut. Normally, he was stronger than almost anyone else I knew, but right now he was limp against the dew-covered ground.

I dropped to my knees next to him and collapsed onto his chest, feeling as though I was moving through the haze of a bad dream. My fingertips were numb as I shook his shoulder.

"Cadmus! Please, wake up," I murmured into his neck.

He smelled so good and familiar as my lips grazed his warm skin, but his dark eyes stayed closed. He didn't even twitch as I kissed first his cheek, then the side of his neck. And in sudden horror, I realized something. No pulse beat beneath my lips.

Frantically, I ran my fingers along his neck and then his wrist, but it was futile. There was nothing there to feel. His heart, so brave and strong, had stopped beating.

I screamed into the night, ripping it apart with my agony as I collapsed once again onto his hard body, clutching him to me as I cried. His handsome face was slack and peaceful and completely unresponsive to my pain. He had been my soul mate for thousands of years, but he was gone from me now. The pain was unbearable and I couldn't even think.

Cool hands grasped my shoulders and tried to pull me away from Cadmus, but I wouldn't have it. I was going nowhere. I clutched his shoulders, breathing him in. I was determined to stay with my husband no matter what. They would have to pry me away.

And then someone did.

Ares pulled me into his strong arms and I clung to him limply as I cried. It didn't seem possible that everything had changed so drastically in the blink of an eye and this unexpected sorrow was debilitating.

"Harmonia."

A voice creaked from the darkness and my sobs froze in my throat as I pulled away from my father and whirled around. Moros' sister stood close by, flanked by the old Keres priest, Annen.

Thanatos. Her name meant death. And while it was true that she could not literally kill an immortal because only Zeus' lost sword could wield that power, she could drain the life from one, leaving him or her lifeless for all of eternity. Which is exactly what she had done to Cadmus.

Before Ares could react, I flew directly at Thanatos' face, scratching and flailing my arms at her. She didn't even try to fend me off. She simply stood, allowing me to pummel her as I screamed. Her bones felt thin and hollow beneath my fists, but her frailty didn't deter me. I wanted her to feel my pain.

"Why?" I screeched, as my left hand connected with the rim of her eye. "Why him? He never did a thing to you!"

Her blood, seeping from her cloudy eyes, was smeared all over my arms and my long evening shift, but it was of no consequence to me. Nothing mattered anymore but hearing her explanation. My eyes were frozen on her ancient face.

"Why?" I demanded again. But she remained frustratingly silent.

"You know why."

The answer came from behind me. I spun to find Moros standing on the edge of the circle, her face a calm mask of perfunctory necessity. Rage exploded within me and I tried to throw myself at her as well, but Ares smoothly caught me, stroking my hair as he held me still.

"Calm yourself, daughter," he murmured into my ear. "It won't bring him back." As he leveled his black gaze at Moros, his voice turned into malicious steel.

"Why have you done this?" he gestured toward my crumpled soul mate and my heart broke into pieces. From behind Ares' thick arm, I glared at Moros with all of the ice I could muster from my frozen heart.

"Why?" she sounded surprised. "Harmonia knows why. I told her a moment ago. According to the prophecy, she will experience a great loss before she seeks Zeus' sword. I have just given her that great loss."

I shrieked again and flailed helplessly against my father as he held me as easily as a rag doll. My mother, however, was not restrained and blurred into motion, instantly standing in front of the old Keres.

"How dare you?" she demanded, with more malice than I had ever heard coming from her lips as her chestnut hair fluttered in the night breeze. Her face, which was perfect in its beauty, was contorted in barely contained rage. "The prophecy does not say that it should be you that brings Harmonia a great loss.

"Do you think that you can meddle with the gods so easily and there will be no consequences? Do you think that Harmonia will find the sword and simply hand it over to you so that you can reign over Olympus, bringing tragedy and sadness to us all? I think not, you ancient hag."

Aphrodite's anger was so great that it fueled the nearby torches and they exploded into the night sky, orange sparks spitting onto the thick damp grass before dying quietly in the dew.

But Moros did not shirk away. She stood hunched as she always did, meeting Aphrodite's unflinching gaze with eyes that were so faded that they seemed strangely opaque. The blood that fell from the corners made her seem that much more grotesque. It dripped down her creased cheeks, running down her arms and streaming into a puddle on the ground around her feet.

She watched Aphrodite silently, something that infuriated my mother even more. Aphrodite lunged at her, grabbing her by the front of her long cloak and hurling the old woman forcefully against a nearby blooming Lotus tree. The Keres collided into the massive trunk and on impact, the brilliant blue Lotus blossoms shriveled and died, falling to the ground in dried black petals.

Moros lay crumpled at the base of the tree, curled into a heap, but her stare was still firm and focused with laser precision on my mother.

"The prophecy is specific," she stated simply, her voice thin and fragile. "Harmonia will suffer a great loss before she finds the sword. It will benefit all of Olympus when she finds it."

"Especially you?" Aphrodite pressed stubbornly. "You feel that you will benefit as you step into your sisters' shoes? Now that we've imprisoned the Fates you think to take their place as the usurping rulers of the Spiritlands in Zeus' absence?" She was so furious that her arms shook and her cheeks flushed in red streaks.

"Aphrodite," Ares interrupted, handing me to my sister Ortrera as he stepped carefully toward my mother. "Be still."

She turned to him in surprise and agitation.

"Be still? You mean… be silent?" Her voice raised an octave. "How dare you? This pathetic heap has rendered your daughter's husband lifeless and you stand idly by and tell me to be silent? This… coming from the god of war? Ppft."

She turned up her nose but gasped as Ares' sword sliced the air directly next to her ear. She whirled, only to find that the sword had impaled one of the many children of the Gorgons.

With the body of a snake and a human head, the creatures were scary enough, but coupled with their ability to turn anyone to stone with their stares, the Gorgons were simply terrifying. This one had wound its way silently from the branches above Aphrodite's head and had been preparing to dangle in front of her, forcing her to meet its deadly gaze. But luckily for her, Ares had seen it first.

As the lifeless Gorgon hung limply from the tree trunk, impaled by Ares' sword, Aphrodite gasped again, staring at the bloody half-reptile. She took a shaking step toward Ares, but she was too slow.

In a blur of motion, he was already standing next to the wounded Keres. Staring down at Moros, his voice boomed like thunder.

"You thought to turn my beloved to stone?"

His voice was as dark as a hurricane and I flinched from the threat that it contained. He lifted a muscled leg and smashed his heavy foot into the old Keres' chest. Her frail bones crunched and I watched her deflate as she wilted into the ground, her ribcage shattered. Her vague moans didn't move me at all. She deserved all of this and more.

Her ragged pants faded into the backdrop of the night as against my will, my gaze sought out my lifeless husband once more.

He lay perfectly still, his beauty unbearable, even in eternal sleep. I collapsed to the ground and scrambled to his side. Curling into him, I held his hand and wept. His limp hand was still warm and I wondered how long it would take before his strong body cooled.

I had never actually seen an immortal rendered lifeless before. I had no way of knowing what to expect. Would he remain just as he was now? Warm and vibrant? I traced the outline of his hand, weaving my fingers through his long ones, wrapping his limp arm around my body.

If I didn't find Zeus' sword, he would remain as this… a lifeless shell of the man that he was. Only the sword could bring him back to me and Zeus could have hidden it anywhere in the world.

The crowd around me was hushed as they waited for me to move. But I didn't. I lay motionlessly with my husband for longer than I knew. As I inhaled his familiar scent, curled into his warm side, I pretended that nothing was wrong…that we were simply laying together as we would any other time. Time passed impotently by. It didn't affect us anymore. We were immortal.

Finally, Aphrodite knelt at my side, her voice gentle.

"Sweetling, let us move Cadmus into the palace. We'll post guards with him. He'll be safe there while we begin our quest for the sword."

"What about the hags?" I whispered, my eyes flitting to the Keres.

Moros was still crumpled on the ground. She hadn't healed yet from her wounds. Each ragged breath she took rasped in her throat and I took joy in that fact. Thanatos

8

hovered near her sister. Her face was unconcerned. She knew her sister would heal quickly. All immortals did. She also knew that she had nothing to fear from us. Only Zeus' sword could truly kill them, just as any other immortal. I swallowed hard.

"Well?" I prompted. "What of the Keres?"

"You know that you hold no power over us," Thanatos uttered. "You cannot do a thing." She turned to my father and pointed a gnarled finger. "Count yourself lucky. There will be no retribution today, war god. But you will not be so lucky next time."

Ares glared at her and took one menacing step, but before he could take another, Thanatos, Moros and Annen were all gone. I glanced around but they were nowhere to be found.

I closed my eyes against the murmuring crowd. I could hear that they were unsettled and afraid, but I couldn't concentrate on that. All I could focus on was my husband's lifeless hand in my lap. I stroked his thumb in the same way that he usually stroked mine.

Bending, I kissed his brow, then his nose, then each closed eyelid. I opened my eyes to study the way his long, dark lashes curled against his cheeks. My heart shattered into pieces and I swallowed hard.

"Sleep tight, my love," I murmured into his ear. "I will undo this. I promise. I love you." I lay with my cheek pressed against his, the wetness from my tears soaking both of us. Finally, my father bent and scooped me up, striding in long steps toward the palace.

"Bring Cadmus," he called over his shoulder to some of the residents swarmed around us. "Carefully."

I closed my eyes and rested against my father's stout chest as he strode purposefully through the courtyard and up the wide marble staircase that led to the back of the palace. I didn't look behind us or in front of us, I simply kept my eyes closed and focused on the strange numbness that was enveloping me.

My husband was the same as dead. It was hard to wrap my mind around. Even though I had lost him in every mortal life that I had been forced by the Fates to live for the past two thousand years, as soon as I returned to the Spiritlands and reclaimed my goddess heritage, I thought I would never have to face this again.

But here we were. My husband was being carried lifelessly to the palace behind me and there wasn't anything I could do. But cry.

CHAPTER TWO

We were surrounded by warriors.

I glanced up with tear soaked cheeks from my bed and gazed woodenly at my half-sister's Amazon warriors who were circling the perimeter of my large, airy bedchamber. Proud and strong, their muscles bulged as they stood at attention, guarding both me and my lifeless husband.

Cadmus lay completely still on a nearby table. As I wept, Aphrodite had covered the long table with cushions and soft blankets before the Olympus residents gently laid Cadmus down on the makeshift bed. His beautiful face was peaceful, as though he slept without a care in the world. His strong hands lay lifelessly at his sides and I wondered where he was. Was his soul simply asleep, waiting for me to wake it? I swallowed hard.

"Ortrera, you do not need to stay in here," I insisted once again to my sister, but I knew that once again she wouldn't listen. She was as head-strong and stubborn as a bull. She stared at me as though I was a child, her brown eyes penetrating mine as she assessed my grief ravaged face.

"Of course we do, Harmonia. I promised father that we would watch you while you slept. I'll also be leaving a handful of warriors to guard Cadmus when we leave in the morning to search for the sword."

I studied the fierce warriors that circled me.

"Who will stay?" I asked quietly. Louder, I added, "Who is willing to protect my husband in my absence?"

Every single warrior raised her hand and stepped forward. A chorus of "I will's" rang throughout my room and my heart warmed a fraction. All of these warriors were brave and loyal. And I knew that each of them would guard Cadmus with her life.

"It's an honor and I thank you," I murmured as I slumped back into my bed, curled onto my side. I numbly watched as Ortrera chose the women who would stay. Four of them stepped forward and stood at attention at each corner of the table Cadmus rested upon. Their fierce, hawk-like faces gave me a small amount of comfort and I closed my eyes to rest.

I had no sooner closed them when I was standing in a blinding, white windstorm. I blinked in confusion against the raging wind and braced myself as I pivoted in a circle. Where was I? God, I hated dreamwalking.

It seemed as though I had been dropped into a winter white-out, a blizzard, yet I didn't feel cold. Everything was black and white at the same time. I couldn't see a thing and my eyes stung from the furious wind gusts. The wind howled and I shivered, not from cold, but from the eeriness surrounding me. It was haunting and frightening, a desolate, barren place. I also recognized a strange heaviness in my arms and legs, as though they were weighted. I felt heavier every moment that I was here, weighing on my chest, making it difficult to breathe. It made me panicky.

"Harmonia!"

Floating to me above the chaos, the familiar deep voice stilled my heart and I whirled, trying to locate my husband. The wind gusts persistently whipped my long hair into my face and I held it out of the way in frustration. I needed to find Cadmus.

And then I did. Keeping his head bowed against the horrid storm, he pushed toward me from what looked like a bleak row of withered trees. I fought to get to him, the churning wind continually holding me back. I struggled onward and within twenty steps, I was in his arms.

"Cadmus!" I cried as I melted into his chest.

His strong arms shielded me from the strange storm and I felt a blissful and wild relief at once again being with him. I was in his arms where I belonged. I glanced up to find his eyes, his normally warm and vivid brown eyes, staring down at me starkly. I startled at his cold expression and drew backward.

"What is it?" I asked, looking around for a threat. "Where are we?"

He shook his head. "I don't know. I was in the courtyard speaking with the Keres and then suddenly, I was here. It seems as though I've been here forever. Time has ceased to exist. How long have I been here?"

"Not long, my love," I murmured into the wind. "Not long at all."

I allowed myself the time to truly examine him and it caused my heart to race. His beautiful face was weary, his eyes hollow. His body was ice cold. As he exhaled, I could see his breath in the air. I gasped. The only other time I had seen that had been with Alexi, the lapdog of the Fates.

"Where are we?" I cried again. "What has happened to you?"

He shook his head sadly. "Harmonia, I don't know. But I don't feel like myself. I feel... dead inside."

"Dead inside? My love..." my voice trailed off. I could see it written all over him. He was emotionless and cold, just as Alexi had been. My Cadmus was gone. It was as though he was… soulless. I froze again.

"Maybe they have your soul," I suggested hesitantly. "Perhaps we are in some strange purgatory."

He stared at me humorlessly. "*I* am in purgatory, you mean. You are not truly here, wife. Thank the gods for that."

And although the words were something that he would normally say, something protective and strong, his tone was flat and cold, as though there was no true emotion behind them. I took a step back. This wasn't truly my husband. This was his body, his shell. His soul was no longer here. The strong heart that I loved so desperately wasn't beating in this cold chest.

He took a look at my face and chuckled a mirthless laugh.

"I know, wife. I don't like me much, either."

"This isn't you," I stuttered. "Cadmus, I will save you. I promise. Somehow I will figure this out and I'll find the sword and I'll bring you back to where you belong. You'll be whole again."

"Will I?" He looked at the white vastness surrounding us. "It doesn't feel as though that will ever be true again."

"I promise you. If it takes every breath in my body, I will save you. You are my life. I don't want to live without you."

He grabbed my wrist with his frigid fingers, his grip pinching my arm.

"Don't say that," he said coldly. "You must live. Regardless of what happens to me. You're too beautiful inside to fade away. But promise me this, wife."

I turned my eyes hesitantly to his cold, beautiful face. I swallowed hard. I knew I wasn't going to like what I heard.

"If this cannot be reversed, find a way to kill me. I do not wish to linger here like this."

He dropped my arm and stared at me blankly. There was nothing in his eyes. Not pain, not desperation, only nothing. Just stark emptiness.

"Promise?" he asked.

I gazed at him wordlessly as horror rose in my chest and I opened my mouth to speak.

And then I was being shaken.

"Harmonia, it is time to go, sweetling."

I opened my eyes to find my mother, Aphrodite, bent over my bed. Her chestnut hair was twisted into a simple knot at her neck and her silvery eyes were gleaming. My gaze flew to the window. Early morning light flooded my room. I had been dreamwalking with Cadmus all night.

The four Amazon warriors stood quietly, still at attention, guarding my empty husband. I knew he was empty, because I knew where he was. I felt a tear slip down my cheek as I scrambled from my bed to where he lay. Unlike in my dream, his body here was warm. It was an enigma. His heart no longer beat, but his body was still warm and unchanged. It was as though he was peacefully sleeping.

But he was empty.

I bent and kissed his soft lips, running my fingers along his chiseled cheekbones.

"Cadmus, I will bring you back to me. I promise."

I held his limp body tightly for a minute more before I flew into action, fluttering around the room readying myself for a journey. I quickly dressed and packed a knapsack. This would be the first time I traveled without Cadmus, a fact that had not slipped past my attention.

When I was ready, I stood in front of the warriors.

"Guard him with your life," I instructed them needlessly. I already knew they would.

"We will,'" the one in front of me confirmed with a nod. I nodded back and met my mother at the door. I glanced over my shoulder only once before we descended the grand staircase to the courtyard below.

Ares, Ortrera and four of her warriors were congregated in the gardens. I overheard them muttering about the box of souls but I was distracted by the number of the warriors.

"Only four?" I asked curiously. Ortrera looked at me once again as though I was a toddler.

"I must leave eight," she explained. "So that Cadmus has a constant guard. My warriors must sleep, too," she added with a small smile.

"Of course," I murmured, feeling foolish. She patted my shoulder in an attempt at sisterly tenderness.

"It is alright, sister. You have much on your mind."

"What were you saying about the box of souls?" I turned to Ares. His expression turned dark as he scowled.

"Somehow, before the Keres disappeared last night, they managed to steal the box of souls from where we were keeping it for Zeus. It must have been Annen."

I thought back and recalled Moros telling me that their ancient priest Annen was performing a task for them. Of course the task had been to hunt for and procure the box of murderous souls. That made perfect sense. My old Aegis, Ahmose, had hidden it for me and I knew that it must have a use, but we hadn't needed it on Ogygia. The box contained every murderous soul that the Keres had ever punished. I had no idea what kind of havoc they could wreak with them.

"Let us think of it later," Aphrodite suggested. "There is no time to address that issue now."

She moved to stand next to Ares and he wrapped his meaty arm around her slender waist. He was wearing war armor, heavy metal plates on his chest and back. They were so heavy that a normal person would never be able to carry them. His jet black hair was freshly washed, still damp in the light of the morning sun. He smiled at me, the tender and loving smile of a father.

"Are you alright, daughter?" he asked.

"No," I admitted. "But I will be eventually."

"We'll find the box," Ares assured me. "And the sword, as well. We will return everything to how it must be. You can count on it."

I nodded silently, assessing the view from the courtyard of Zeus' palace. The gardens were in full bloom this morning, brilliant blossoms of every hue hanging over our heads, lining the walkways and filling the courtyard with heavy floral scents. Lilies, honeysuckle, jasmine, roses. I let the sweet smells fill my mouth as I breathed them in.

The city below us was quiet, as though the residents knew that things had changed so completely. No one traveled on the cobblestone streets and the normal hustle and bustle of the city was gone. The shops and marketplaces were empty. If anyone remained in the city, they were safely ensconced in their homes.

"I saw Cadmus in the night," I stated simply, my back still to my parents. I heard Aphrodite's quick intake of breath before she flew to my side, her cool hand on my elbow.

"Where is he?" she asked hesitantly. I could feel her silver goddess stare on my face, but I kept my gaze on the silent city below us. If I looked into her concerned eyes, I might cry again.

"I don't know," I sighed. "Somewhere I've never been before. It seemed like a horrible purgatory and he wasn't the same. He wasn't Cadmus. I think they have his soul trapped somewhere."

Ares stared at me, his black stare unflinching. "Our first stop is with Hecate. We shall see if she knows anything about this place."

I thought of Hecate. It had been she, the goddess of witchcraft, who had pulled us safely out of Ogygia when we confronted the Fates and the Keres. Calypso's island quickly pulled visitors into a blissful, unaware state where time was no longer relevant. If it hadn't been for Hecate, we would all still be on the island, completely unaware of anything.

I nodded. Of course Hecate should be our first stop. She knew things that we did not. They simply appeared to her in visions. If anyone would know of the strange purgatory, it would be her or her sidekicks, Circes and Medea.

I lifted my head at Ortrera's shrill whistle and watched her fleet of Pegasus' descending upon us from the sky. They were truly a sight to behold. A herd of magnificent mares of every color, each of their faces was painted with war paint. Their large wings pulsed quickly, radiating strength as they glided to a smooth landing in the courtyard next to us. They stood still now, perfectly trained as the war horses that they were.

I walked around the lead horse, the one that I would share with Ortrera, and rested my cheek against her solid, warm neck. She didn't move, she just absorbed my weight, letting me rest against her soft, sleek fur. My mind was numb and I let it wander, thinking of just yesterday when Cadmus and I had spent the afternoon feeding each other Lotus blossoms by a bubbling stream.

"Sister?" Ortrera inquired, her eyebrows raised. She stood next to her horse, ready to mount. Her bow and arrows were strapped to her back, a long dagger at her thick, muscled waist. "Are you ready?"

"I'm ready," I nodded. "Let us leave here."

Everyone mounted and I clung to Ortrera's strong back as the horses flew into the sky. I absently observed the Spiritlands below us as we flew toward Hecate's cave by the border. There was scarcely any life to be found, it was as though everyone in the land had gone into hiding. They probably had. They didn't know what was coming and honestly, neither did I.

Within twenty minutes, I spotted the cave and the horses began their rapid descent. As usual, Hecate was waiting for us in the doorway because she had felt us drawing near. Her magic was unsettling at best.

"Harmonia, how are you holding up?" she asked in concern, her beautiful face twisted into a scowl. "Blast the Keres, anyway. What did Ares do to them?"

"Nothing," he admitted, his shoulders slumping slightly. "They disappeared into the night. But there will be a reckoning, I can assure you of that."

She nodded, satisfied that he was telling the truth. No one could doubt it. The look on his fierce face was sharp and determined. He was the god of war, after all.

"Come in," she invited, ushering us into her home.

We walked past her into the brilliantly gleaming cave. Every wall and every surface was filled with glittering white stalactites and stalagmites. It looked ethereal, not what you would expect a gateway to Hades to be. It was rumored that there was a direct path to the underworld from this very cave, although I had never confirmed it. Since one of the duties that Hecate had been given included ushering demons to hell, it just made sense that the rumors were true.

Hecate turned to me now, compassion apparent on her lovely features. While Medea and Circes often appeared as ancient hags, Hecate always appeared as a young, beautiful woman. Her lips always gleamed crimson, her blonde hair always fell in long ringlets down her back.

"How are you, really?" she asked me softly, placing a hand on my shoulder.

A lump formed in my throat and I thought about telling her that truth... that my world had fallen apart in the space of a minute. But there was no need. Anyone who knew me was already perfectly aware of that.

"I'm holding up," I said simply. She nodded, leading the way to an inner room of her cave- a place I had never been.

We ducked through a doorway and stood in a black abyss. The walls in here were gleaming black crystal but instead of reflecting light, they appeared to absorb it, to suck it in.

"Fire," Hecate murmured, and a large ring of blue flame appeared in the center of the cavernous room.

I watched the flickering fire in fascination. It burned with jewel-like colors- blue, green and turquoise, while it shimmered with metallic light.

"Follow me," Hecate instructed and she stepped through the flame and stood in the center of the blazing ring.

With hesitation, I did the same. I was surprised to find that the flame didn't burn me. It was cool to my touch. I turned and held my hand out to my mother. She was apprehensive, but obligingly stepped through, quickly crossing to my side and grasping my hand tightly. Ares and the Amazons rapidly crossed into the circle, exhibiting no fear. That didn't surprise me; they never allowed their nervousness to show.

"Hold hands," Hecate instructed, closing her eyes.

She began murmuring things that I didn't understand and I felt a strange vagueness filtering through my body. My arms and legs felt light and airy and I began to feel as though I would float away if it weren't for Ares on my left and Aphrodite on my right weighting me down. The sensation was a curious one.

Hecate's mutterings became more and more insistent and loud until it reached a feverish pitch and she was shouting in a strange guttural language that I had never heard before.

She began nodding quickly and whispered, "A sword, a sword, a sword."

She rocked to and fro, still nodding, practically humming the words. "A sword, a sword, a sword."

And then she stopped and added, "In a stone. A sword in a stone."

She went completely still and in the silence of the vast room, a vision suddenly filled my head, a vision so vivid that it took my breath away and caused me to close my eyes in order to focus on it.

A magnificent waterfall cascaded into a clear and sparkling lake. The sun hit the water and reflected into the sky in a million glittering prisms as the crash of the mighty waterfall fed it. At the top, rushing water spilled over large stone boulders covered in velvety green moss in a mad frenzy. A bone-handled sword was firmly embedded in one of the stones. It stood tall and proud, unmoved by the furious crashing of the water against it.

A sword in a stone. Deep within my belly, recognition grew, larger and larger until I pinpointed it and couldn't deny it. I knew this place. I had been there before.

Camelot.

CHAPTER THREE

I sucked in my breath and Hecate's eyes popped open, meeting mine.

"A sword in a stone," she repeated. "You know of it."

I could feel everyone's eyes upon me as I nodded. "Yes. I've been there before. Was I the only one who saw the vision?"

I scanned the circle and found the same blank look on everyone else's face. I was the only one who had seen it. But I wasn't the only one who had been there before. I squeezed my mother's hand.

"You've been there, too. And Ares. And... Cadmus." I gulped. "I know where Zeus hid the sword. The question is... how do we get to it? It was removed long ago and according to legend, it has never been found again."

"Ah, Harmonia," Hecate clucked. "You know it is no legend. Camelot existed and you lived there. And the answer is clear. To get to it, you must return to where you know it is."

At my blank look, she sighed. "You must travel back to when you were there before."

My heart thrilled in my chest at the idea. Nothing else mattered except for the fact that Cadmus was there. Alive and well, with his heart still beating, his body still warm and strong. Somewhere, far from here, my soul mate was waiting for me. All I had to do was return to him. I clutched the bloodstone that hung motionlessly from my neck. Throughout the ordeal of this past day, I hadn't given my pendant much thought. But it still did contain great power. It was, after all, created from the blood of Zeus himself.

"How?" I whispered. "How do I get there?" The words stumbled out haltingly as I fingered the cool stone of my necklace. Electricity jolted through my fingers and I felt my eyes glaze over.

Hecate watched me, her face thoughtful.

"Harmonia, you realize of course, that you will be returning for a purpose. You will not be returning to stay. Do you understand?"

I almost didn't hear her as my mind was flooded with images of the past. Once again, as it had done so many times before, my bloodstone was giving me glimpses of a past life. Cadmus had been a knight. A chivalrous, beautiful knight. Visions of his gleaming silver armor filled my mind, his smile beckoning me from beneath the visor of his helmet.

"Harmonia?" Aphrodite prompted. "Come back to us."

I shook the memories from my head and re-focused on my mother.

"Mother, Hecate is correct. Camelot existed and we were there. We must return there to retrieve the sword. It is the only way."

Aphrodite nodded solemnly, perfectly willing to do anything required of her. History had always portrayed her as superficial and flighty, but truly that perception couldn't be further from the truth. Yes, she was dramatic and colorful, but she was thoughtful and strong, as well.

"Fine. We travel. Tell me, though, how do we get to the sword?" Ares' voice boomed in the delicate, crystal room. The Amazons were all nodding. They were less concerned with our predicament once we got there and more focused on simply getting on with it, just as Ares was.

Hecate smiled at their impatience.

"Your warriors cannot accompany you," she told me gently. "Only the three of you. The Amazons were not there originally, so they cannot be there now."

She nodded her head toward the warriors and after a curt nod from Ortrera, they obligingly stepped from the circle.

"Father, if you need me, send for me," Ortrera said hesitantly. "It does not feel right to let you go alone."

Ares gazed at his warrior daughter. "You make me proud, Ortrera. Rest assured, all will be well."

"Watch over Cadmus, please, sister," I requested softly. Her eyes softened.

"You know that I will, Harmonia," she replied gently. "He will never be alone. He will be safe and sound when you return."

"In order to return, you must first leave," Hecate observed drily. "We are wasting time here. Hold hands again."

She crossed from her place and moved to me, placing her hands upon mine and looking into my eyes. Hers glimmered deep and blue, reflecting the flickering flame around us. It was mesmerizing.

"Harmonia, Cadmus is not well right now. His soul is lost and the only hope of saving him is Zeus' sword. You must not become entrenched in your life in Camelot, because as all mortal lives, it is fleeting and temporary.

"And of course, as always, the Fates put you in a tragic position. Do not become fooled. You won't like your ending there anymore than you enjoy your current situation here. You must recover the sword and bring it back here in order to save us all, Cadmus included."

I nodded. "I saw him in a dream. His eyes were so cold and empty…" my voice trailed off.

"He *is* empty," Hecate confirmed. "He is not in Hades, but the Wasteland where he is being held is almost worse, it is neither here, nor there, nor Hades. It's just a land full of nothing, a place created by the Keres' as a holding place for horrific souls. They keep them there until they need them, just as they needed Alexi. While Cadmus is there, he knows how he should feel, but he can't truly feel it. Feelings are gone from him, just like his soul. Do everything you can to set it right."

As if I could do anything else. This was my soul mate that we were talking about. A thought suddenly occurred to me, freezing the breath on my lips.

"Hecate," I began hesitantly. "Cadmus' soul. The Keres have taken it and they have also taken the Box of Souls back. Is his soul in the box? Will we need to find the box before Cadmus is saved by the sword?"

Hecate nodded. "I believe so. I can't be certain, but it appears that way."

I found it suddenly hard to swallow. So, it wasn't enough that the Keres had rendered Cadmus lifeless. My husband's soul was somewhere out there in a box of murderous souls. My tongue felt like lead as I tried to speak. I licked my lips and tried again.

"Ares…"

He moved to my side in a blur of motion.

"They will pay," the god of war promised me firmly, knowing what I was trying to ask him. "I will make sure of it."

I nodded, tampering the bloodthirsty feelings back down. I didn't care what their motives were at this point-whether the Keres were selfless or selfish. They had no right to use Cadmus as leverage. I would personally stand over them as Ares' gouged their eyes out and fed them to the ravens.

"Let's go," I whispered, holding tightly to my father's strong arm. "Let us just go. I must help Cadmus."

We rejoined hands and I gripped my bloodstone, feeling the familiar electric pulse as Hecate once again chanted. My limbs grew weak and images flitted in and out of my mind like puzzle pieces. The energy threw my head back and everything went black as a sensation almost too much to bear overwhelmed me. We were suddenly spinning as we rocketed through the blackness of time at incredible speed before everything halted with an abrupt jolt.

Time travel was exquisite and confusing at once. Our souls were thrust into our previous bodies with no aplomb whatsoever. It took a moment to adjust.

I could hear the noisy racket and clanging dinnerware before I even opened my eyes. As my lashes fluttered open, I found myself in the midst of an elaborate banquet in the center of a massive dining hall. I glanced down at myself and discovered that I was clothed in medieval clothing, a long sweeping red velvet dress with an empire waist, corded in elaborate golden strands. The odd thing was that I vividly remembered this dress. It had been one of my favorites. It looked striking with my long dark hair.

Aphrodite was seated next to me, dressed similarly, although as Queen Guinevere, she was wearing a simple crown. She was attired in blue, with a heavy matching sapphire necklace and earrings. Her silver goddess eyes were gone, replaced by sparkling dark ones. As my eyes flew around the room, memories from this life returned to me, rapidly fitting themselves into my consciousness as though they had been there all along.

I remembered being here as though it was yesterday and even though I had been through this process before in ancient Alexandria, I couldn't get used to the overwhelming sense of déjà vu. Once here, the memories from my life in the Spiritlands became muted and distant, as though I looked at them from a dream. My new reality became the one I was immersed in. I was going to have to consciously remind myself of my purpose.

King Arthur himself sat at the head of the banquet table. He ate in between talking with boisterous laughs and wild hand gestures. He was a huge personality. When he entered a room, he owned it. His dark blonde curls fell casually against his neck, his eyes cornflower blue. He was a handsome man, kind and strong.

My father was seated next to him in Lancelot's chair. As the King's champion, Lancelot was always near the King. I found him holding my gaze and I stared into his dark eyes. He looked to my mother and waggled his eyebrows and I swallowed a laugh. One thing about my father, he was always able to joke… that is, until it was time to kill someone.

All around us, members of King Arthur's court laughed and danced and ate. Pheasant, curried sweet potato, roast pig and vegetables lined every table and sweet mead flowed freely in heavy mugs. Thick tapestries covered the stone walls, insulating the interior from the dampness of the outdoors, while the floors were scuffed by the heavy chairs lining each table.

I was so entranced with studying my surroundings that I momentarily forgot to look for Cadmus until his husky whisper resounded in my ear.

"Would you like to walk with me, my love?"

I spun in my chair, my jaw dropping at the sight of him. He wore a flowing white shirt and snug linen trousers and his smile lit up the room. His dark hair and eyes were the same as they were in every life, and I ached to reach my hand out and touch his tanned face.

"Lucan."

His name somehow formed on my tongue as though it had been there all along. But then I was at a loss for something to say. I couldn't tell him anything that was on my mind. As far as he knew, he was Sir Lucan, a Knight from King Arthur's roundtable and I was Heleyne, a lady –in-waiting to Queen Guinevere. If I said anything to the contrary, he would think I had been bewitched, a fate considered worse than death here.

"Yes?" he waited flirtatiously. He studied my face.

"You were going to say, 'Yes, Lucan, my handsome amazing Knight, I would love to walk with you?" he prompted then grinned and I couldn't help but smile. It was so good to see Cadmus alive and well. His cockiness was a trait that he retained in every single life.

"Okay," I nodded. "I'll walk with you."

"Your enthusiasm is contagious, my lady," he mumbled as he helped me rise from my chair. I beamed at him and rephrased.

"Sir Lucan, I am most excited to walk with you, I assure you. You are the strongest and most handsome knight in all of the land. What woman would not be excited with your mere presence?"

He laughed as he grasped my elbow, leaning in to whisper into my ear.

"You're a cheeky thing," he said, before gently guiding me through the crowded room. As we passed through the heavy double doors and into the damp stone hallways, the flute playing grew muted, as did the din of voices.

The stone bricks of the palace kept the interior cool and after night fell, it actually became quite chilly. I shivered and leaned into Lucan's warm body as we walked. I felt him grin as he tightened his arm around my shoulders.

The green crest of Arthur Pendragon hung clearly in the massive entry hall for everyone to see and for most, it was a welcome sight. Arthur had truly given Camelot hope and had quickly become a beloved king. He was a kind, just man who had given the country something that they had previously lacked- a fair ruler. The prior king, Arthur's biological father Uther, had ruled with fear.

Lucan dipped his head again, his lips brushing against my ear.

"I thought about you today, my lady, when I was supposed to be jousting."

The thought of his mind wandering while long sharp objects were trying to knock him off his horse alarmed me.

"Luc, you've got to be careful! I have no wish to see you injured," I chided and as I did, I once again felt as though I had never left this place, as though I had been in Camelot all along. It was so easy to pick up where I had left off and I saw now why Hecate had felt it necessary to issue a warning.

It would be so easy to want to remain here… to brush aside all responsibility and fear from my present life and just stay here in Camelot where currently everything was perfect. But I knew all too well, that even if I didn't remember exactly how just yet, both Lucan and I would die young and tragically here. The Fates had ensured that, time and time again. But it was so very easy to block that out when Lucan was smiling at me so vibrantly.

"But where is the fun in that?" he laughed, throwing his head back. "Since when are you such a worrier?"

"Since... never," I admitted. "I don't usually need to. You are competent and strong. But I have no wish to see you bloodied on the field, Lucan. You're much too pretty to be bloody."

I reached out and stroked his face and he leaned into my hand.

"Knights are not pretty, my lady," he said sternly, clasping me to him.

"Oh?" I raised my eyebrows. "I beg to differ. You are both beautiful and a knight, so you are wrong. Knights can be pretty."

We stepped out of the palace doors and into the lush grass walkway that led up to the palace gardens. Dew was already forming on the grass and I felt it saturate my thin satin slippers. The air was damp, so much so that I could feel moisture forming on my skin like wet velvet.

Lucan led me to a nearby stone bench situated just off the beaten path and in the shadows. If I were alone, I would never have ventured into the dark in such a way. It simply wasn't safe. But Lucan was just as deadly in this life as he was in every other one in which he'd ever lived. I was safer with him than anywhere else in the world.

I melted against him as we sat, enjoying his masculine scent and the strength that ebbed from him almost palpably. It didn't matter what his name was or which body he inhabited, he was always the same person and it was my sole mission now to save him.

"It's a beautiful night, is it not?" he drawled as he stared up at the black night, stretching before he dropped his arm around my back in a subtle gesture as old as time. The bright stars twinkled and I couldn't help but enjoy being here with him, in spite of the pressing responsibility that I felt to find the sword. I could take just a moment to enjoy him. What would it hurt?

"Will you come to my chambers tonight?" I murmured against his neck.

"Has there been a night in your most recent memory when I have not?" he stared at me incredulously.

"Not that I recall," I laughed softly, enjoying his long fingers wrapped in mine as I ran my fingers through his silky dark hair.

"Well, then there is no reason to begin now," he announced with finality.

He lowered his head and engulfed my mouth with his own. I could taste the honeyed mead on his lips and I drew him even closer, clutching at his strong back. I would never be able to get close enough to him, but I could certainly try.

As his mouth made love to mine, I found myself wondering about our future here. Would I be gone before Lucan died in this life? Because I certainly did not want to witness that yet again. I had lost him too many times already.

But as he deepened the kiss even further, I shoved the unpleasant thoughts from my mind. I was here now and so was he. I'd think about the ugliness later and simply enjoy the now.

CHAPTER FOUR

I couldn't sleep. I tossed and turned in the lavishly adorned bed, twisting about in the soft bedclothes, but slumber just wouldn't come to me. Finally, after staring at the stone ceiling for half an hour more, I crawled out of bed with a sigh. There was no reason to keep Lucan awake with my restlessness.

I glanced over my shoulder at him. He looked like a little boy as he slept, his handsome face slack and relaxed. I smiled to myself. I couldn't get over having him back. Time travel was truly a miracle and a blessing. If I blocked out reality just enough, I could pretend that everything was fine.

I pulled a lacy silk wrap over my nightgown and slipped soundlessly onto my balcony. Leaning onto the thick stone ledge, I stared absently at the countryside below me. Even at night, Camelot was beautiful. Wild bramble and bluebells adorned the rolling hills, along with brilliant red poppies and dark purple violets, appearing as a scene from a vivid painting. I could only just make out the colors in the darkness because of the full yellow moon that hung on the horizon.

The nighttime dew was so thick that it formed on my own skin within a few minutes. It rained quite a lot here. But the rain kept everything fresh and new, kept the grasses thick and lush. It also made the air clean and sweet. I inhaled a deep breath. It smelled like a mountain spring would taste.

Lucan stirred in his sleep and I turned, watching him bury his head deep under the pillows through the fluttering curtains surrounding my bed. They were more prone to heavy velvet draperies here in Camelot, but I had insisted on gauzy sheer curtains in my bedchambers. I supposed it was a throwback to my true heritage in the Spiritlands. The weather was perfect there, so we had no need for heavy cloth. We had the luxury of beauty over functionality.

I sighed as I realized that if I was comparing the Spiritlands to Camelot, then I was truly wide awake. I knew I was not going back to sleep now. And if I was going to be awake, I might as well reacquaint myself with the castle. We were here on a mission and failure was not an option. I could sleep when we returned to the Spiritlands. I quietly crept past my bed where Lucan blissfully slept and slipped silently out into the hall, closing the door softly behind me.

The corridors were cool and shadowy, the light from the flickering torches slowly dying. My nose twitched as I sniffed at the lamp oil. They would just barely last until morning, each hour burning lower and lower until they burned out just as they sun came up. Like everything else in Camelot, they did their jobs perfectly. Arthur made sure that everything worked like a well-oiled machine.

As I walked, I trailed my fingers along the rough-hewn blocks of the walls. How could I ever have forgotten this life? It was astounding to me that the Fates had truly held that much power over me. They had literally played games with my mind and I had allowed it. *Never again*, I vowed to myself, as I turned a darkened corner.

A flicker of movement stilled my footsteps and out of instinct, I stepped back into the cover of darkness. With interest, I watched a figure emerge from the king's bedchambers and then I saw Guinevere's face in the dim torchlight. I sighed in relief. Sleep was alluding her, as well, and it would give me a chance to speak with her.

I moved toward her, but something was wrong and I froze once again in the shadows. A dark light shimmered over her body, flickering and swirling up and down the length of her. It made her appear as a mirage. I blinked my eyes closed, but she was the same when I reopened them.

And then she was no longer my mother. Her body twisted and contorted and she morphed into Morgan le Fey, the half-sister of the king. She stood quietly for a moment, completely still. But while her dark blue eyes stared straight ahead, I was able to see something within them.

She was Eris. Morgan was actually Eris, the goddess of strife and discord- my polar opposite. She had been a thorn in my side for several millennia and she had never been more devious than she was as Morgan.

In fascination, I watched her catch her breath, lifting a shaking hand to tuck a long tendril of dark hair out of her face. Eris had kidnapped Cadmus in the Spiritlands- feeding him a love potion to make him think that he loved her. I never had a chance to confront her about that because the Fates had enslaved her and in fact, that was where she currently was now—trapped in an empty fire pit with them on Calypso's island. My fingers itched to carry out vengeance on this version of Eris… to scratch Morgan le Fey's eyes out- to use my goddess strength and hurl her from the nearest balcony.

But I did not. I clenched my hands tightly at my sides instead, knowing that I was likely drawing blood with my fingernails. Contempt filled me up and I had to literally fight with myself to contain it.

What was Morgan doing in Arthur's chamber? Especially disguised as my mother? And then realization, a dark, hideous theory, dawned on me and I swallowed my own bile. Surely, even Eris wouldn't... surely not. She didn't sleep with her own brother disguised as Guinevere. That would be positively the worst thing I had ever known her to do.

But I knew that she was agitated with him. She and Arthur Pendragon shared the same mother. It was his father, Uther, who had the royal blood and Morgan had always resented him for that. When I was here last, I suspected her of sabotaging the king, but it had not been her who had ultimately done it. Or had she? Had she been involved all along?

The heavy bedchamber door interrupted my musings as it creaked open once again and Arthur stepped into the hall, his face flushed and golden hair disheveled.

"Ginny," he began, using his pet name for Guinevere.

But at his voice, Morgan turned and Arthur saw her face- dressed in exactly the same clothing that he had just seen his wife wearing. The wife that he thought he had just made love to. If I had doubted that before, the look on his face clarified it for me.

"What the..." he stuttered, reaching out to touch the hem of her nightgown's bell sleeve. Confusion spun across his face and then revulsion as he realized the depths of his sister's treachery. He took an automatic step backward. I imagined that his face mirrored my own from a moment ago, the picture of absolute horror.

"Morgan..." he began and then trailed off. "What is the meaning of this?"

One thing about Arthur, regardless of the many times Morgan had given him pause or reason to doubt her, he always believed the best in her, as well as everyone else. He knew, along with the rest of the kingdom, that his sister had witch-like tendencies but he overlooked them out of loyalty to her. His idealistic ideas would eventually be his undoing. His good heart just couldn't fathom that darkness truly did exist.

Morgan laughed and I heard Eris in the evil cackle that resonated down the empty hall. I flinched away from it as my heart broke for Arthur. He loved Guinevere to distraction. This would kill him and his face already spoke to that.

"What have you done to me?" he whispered. "Why?"

She shrugged her bony shoulders. "Why not? You do not deserve all that you have, dear brother. Why does the simple matter of paternity determine our greatness? We share the same mother, yet you are king. How is that fair?"

"That is simply the way things are, Morgan," he stated wearily. "You know that it is not something that I control."

"No," she sneered. "But as king, you control everything else in this land. However, if your beloved subjects ever discover that you had a love affair with your very own sister, I fear that they shall turn from you, brother."

She pasted an innocent look onto her face and I wanted to vomit.

"You wouldn't," Arthur uttered. "Why would you?"

"Don't ever say that I *wouldn't*," Morgan smiled evilly. "Trust me, I would."

Arthur was speechless as he stared at his sister. I saw every emotion possible roll across his face…betrayal, disgust, sadness. Morgan leaned forward, peering into the darkness. She shook her head in frustration and snapped her fingers. The torch nearest to her exploded into flames, licking at the stone wall.

Arthur gasped and I realized that while Morgan might not realize her true identity, she had certainly learned to tap into at least some of her goddess powers. My air sucked out of me. Perfect. I would have an unbalanced psychopath on my hands armed with immortal supernatural power. This night kept getting better and better.

"What, brother?" she grinned. "I just wanted to see your handsome face more clearly." She stepped forward and trailed her fingers lightly across his cheek. He flinched away from her.

"What?" she whispered into his ear as she ran her other hand across his chest. "You didn't mind my touch a few minutes ago."

"I thought you were my wife," he spit angrily. "Everyone knows of my love for Guinevere. No one will believe you."

"They'll believe their own eyes, brother," she replied, pulling something out of her robe pocket. Opening her hand, she revealed a small crystal globe. Tossing it onto the stone floor, it shattered and dark blue smoke filled the corridor. Out of the wispy tendrils, two figures emerged. Arthur and Morgan.

Clearly she had contrived this illusion, but it was very convincing as I watched the two smoky figures embrace. Reaching for each other, they kissed and allowed their hands to roam freely over each other's body. Once again, I had to swallow my revulsion. As the two figures tumbled to the floor lovingly, I closed my eyes.

"If you performed such a trick for anyone else, you would be burned as a witch," Arthur said calmly as we watched the illusion fade away. "Would you risk that?"

She laughed once again, a chilling, horrible sound. "You have no idea of the lengths I would go," she replied.

Arthur's shoulders slumped. There was no doubting the determined, unhinged look on Morgan's face.

"What do you want from me?" he asked dejectedly.

"I'll get back to you on that," she promised. "Trust me."

And she was gone. I glanced up and down the hall, but she had simply disappeared. I sighed. I still hated it when people did that. It was unsettling.

Arthur leaned against the wall for a moment, drawing in deep breaths and I found myself desperately wanting to hug him. He had been instantly immersed in madness and treachery. Most mortals would lose their minds. But he was strong and I watched him square his shoulders as he returned to his bedchambers.

I was just about to turn away as well and creep back to my own chambers, when I felt someone's stare between my shoulder blades.

I turned and found Merlin, the king's oldest advisor, standing in another darkened alcove. I could tell from his face that he had witnessed the same thing that I had. His wizened face was blank, but his eyes were bothered. And his eyes are what held me tightly to the ground- they were jet black and glittering from the shadows.

They were eyes that I had seen a thousand times before.

He was Ahmose.

CHAPTER FIVE

I almost moved to meet him at goddess speed, but reminded myself that he didn't know that I was now aware of who I truly was. It was difficult, but I forced my feet to walk at the slower mortal pace, meeting him in the middle of the great hall. The last time I had seen him had been when the Fates had tortured him to his death, something that he was not aware of now. It was mind bending.

"My lady," he nodded curtly. "What brings you out at this hour?"

"I couldn't sleep, Ahmose," I murmured.

"Never call me that here," he reprimanded sternly. "You know that I am Merlin. Do not be so careless, Heleyne."

On his face, I saw almost fatherly concern and I wished that I had noticed it in other lives. I had always been annoyed by him, by his vague answers to my questions. I never knew that that he had been a simple pawn to the Fates. None of it had been his fault... and he had eventually given his life to save me.

I swallowed hard.

"What troubles you?" he asked. "Is everything well with Lucan? With the queen?"

I nodded. "Everything is well," I whispered.

"Then why do I see clouds on your face?" he asked. His eyes were razor sharp. They missed nothing, a fact that I regretted right now. How was I going to get anything past him? He'd known me for several millennia.

"I'm fine," I murmured. "Just tired."

He seemed to consider that, staring at me thoughtfully. I had to admit, it was strange to see him without his customary dark robes. As Merlin, he was wearing typical woolen pants, an embroidered shirt and a simple cloak. His ancient face was free of cosmetics- free from the black eye makeup that he usually favored.

"Things are moving forward," he observed, his eyes gazing over as he reflected. "The witch has tricked Arthur. Do you know what to do now?"

His gaze flickered to the Phoenix birthmark on my wrist. For thousands of years, the Fates had allowed me to believe that it marked me as a Keeper for them, meaning that I was meant to keep their grand plans. But in reality, it marked me as the Chosen One, the one who would eventually right the wrongs of Fate. I had only discovered this recently, after Ahmose had died.

I nodded. I did remember from my first time here.

"Yes. Guinevere must draw closer to Lancelot. I don't think that will be a problem."

I considered my parents. Keeping them apart was definitely not a problem.

Merlin smiled. "Go back to bed then, little keeper. We have much work ahead of us in the near future."

I turned and began my trip down the darkened hall, not stopping until I reached the opposite end. I glanced over my shoulder, but Merlin was already gone. I crept back to my room and silently slipped into bed with Lucan. He still slept blissfully unaware of the peril that we were faced with in our true lives. I sighed and closed my eyes.

* * *

Something tickled my face and I cringed, turning into my pillows. Through my eyelids, I felt the light invading my room and I was not in the mood for it. I had never been what you could honestly consider a morning person.

"Wake up, beautiful," Lucan murmured into my ear.

My eyes popped open.

His handsome face hovered over mine, his hair dangling into my face. I reached up and tucked it behind his ear as he dipped his head and kissed me.

After I caught my breath, I murmured, "Aren't you supposed to be with the other men?" The knights from the Roundtable spent every morning jousting, running drills and performing strength training.

"Are you saying that I'm a layabout?" he asked with a grin. As always, his smile took my breath away and I inhaled a shaky breath.

"Of course not, my love," I assured him. "I'm just surprised to find you still here. You're usually long gone by the time I wake."

"So, then, who is the layabout?" he teased, stroking my arm lightly.

I watched the sun's rays bathe him as he moved and was hard-pressed to decide who shone more brightly: Lucan or the actual sun. He twisted into a sitting position, reaching over to grab his shirt from the nightstand.

"Must you go?" I whispered. He looked at me questioningly.

"Of course, my sweet. There are things to be done. But I shall see you later today," he promised. He finished dressing as I watched and dipped to kiss me goodbye.

"I'll see you at dinner," he murmured, his lips grazing my cheek.

And then he was gone. I dropped back onto the pillows with a sigh. I could stay with him all day long and never complain. Once I returned to the Spiritlands with the sword and brought Cadmus back to me, I vowed to do just that. I would never let him out of my sight again.

I dressed myself in another heavy velvet gown, pulling my hair into a simple knot at the nape of my neck and shoving my feet into thin slippers. After applying lip stain to my lips, I left my chambers in search of my mother.

The halls of the palace were bustling now, a far cry from the emptiness that I had encountered last night. House servants rushed about cleaning, delivering fresh linen and laying clean rushes on the floors. Every window was wide open and the fresh air blew gently through the corridors. I glanced down from one of them, absently scanning the gardens below, and was surprised to find my mother and father sequestered in a dark nook in the courtyard.

I shook my head in annoyance. What were they thinking? If I could see them, anyone looking down from this level could. I picked up my pace and worked my way down to the ground floor as quickly as I could, being careful to not trip on my long skirts.

Rushing around the final corner, I found that they were still together. My father had her smashed against his hard chest and was stroking one large hand through her hair, all the while staring lovingly into her eyes. My ire rose even higher, but to my frustration, I found that I wasn't the only one that had discovered them.

Across the courtyard, in another darkened nook, I saw someone else, a man who I didn't know, watching the queen and Lancelot with interest as he peeled an apple. His dark eyes met mine from across the courtyard and a tiny smile tilted his lips as he gave me a small salute, the knife still in his hands.

My pulse took off like a rocket and I hurried to where my mother and father stood.

"What are you doing?" I hissed. "Anyone can see you- in fact, someone has!"

Lancelot seemed unconcerned as he glanced around.

"Where, daughter?" he asked. "I see no one."

I pointed into the direction of the stranger and stopped. My father was correct. The stranger was gone. My heart continued to beat furiously in my chest.

"What if he goes straight to Arthur?" I asked anxiously. "You cannot be found out this way."

"Or what?" he leveled a calm gaze at me. "You are still thinking as though you are a Keeper of Fate. You know that you are not," he admonished. "We do not bow to the whims of the Fates."

"Ares," my mother interrupted gently, laying a hand on his arm. "There is no reason to change anything that happened here. We should do our best to simply find the sword and leave this place as we found it."

She looked lovely today in a peach colored flaunt and ivory underskirt. The overskirt was delicately threaded with webs of tiny pearls. An external corset was tightly laced up at the back and I had to wonder if my father had helped her dress this morning, since I knew that I had not. Her chestnut hair gleamed in the light as she ducked her head toward me, ignoring Lancelot's grumblings.

"I'm sorry, my sweet," she apologized, reaching out to stroke my cheek. "We didn't think that anyone could see us. We'll be more careful."

"That is the problem," I muttered. "You didn't think. And please don't refer to my father as Ares. He is Lancelot here."

She smiled good-naturedly, not bringing up the fact that here in Camelot, she was queen and I should not be so mouthy. She was accustomed to my cheekiness, however. I had never managed to overcome it in any life that we had ever lived.

She linked her arm with mine. "Come," she soothed me. "Let us find some breakfast." I allowed her to lead me from the flowering gardens, but I couldn't resist a parting shot at my father.

"You're late for morning drills," I called over my shoulder. I could hear him laughing as we rounded the corner and I rolled my eyes.

My mother and I made our way to the main banquet hall, smiling at each curtsying well-wisher along the way. Everyone in this kingdom was enamored with Guinevere. As always, she had retained her customary charm in this life. Most people clamored to please her.

As we passed through the heavy double doors, I took in the festive breakfast atmosphere. The long tables were lined with rows of candles, ribbons and vivid purple violets, King Arthur's favorite. The candles were as yet unlit- they would be saved for dinner this evening. There were also massive chandeliers made from candles hanging over head, ready for lighting at night fall. Right now, though, the morning sun provided quite enough light, even in this darkened room.

Guinevere took a seat and before she could even move, servants had rushed to provide her with silverware, a linen napkin and a plate of steaming breakfast. I shook my head. It wasn't merely the fact that she was queen that made people fall in love with her. It was her charm, *Aphrodite's* charm. She smiled a brilliant grin at the servant in front of her and dug into her plate with relish.

I waited patiently for mine to arrive, which it did several minutes after Guinevere's. Soft white bread, thick peppered bacon slices and warm venison were piled high on the pewter plate in front of me and my mouth watered. I was ravenous.

What I wouldn't give for some nectar from the Spiritlands, but I settled instead for tepid milk in a heavy mug. Thick cream topped it off and I felt the cool foam stick to my upper lip. My breakfast wasn't ambrosia and nectar, but it would do.

As I gazed thoughtfully around the room, I examined the servants bustling about. They all had contented expressions on their faces. They were happy to be working for Arthur, relieved to be safe within the protection of his castle. The kingdom outside of these walls was in a state of unrest and had been for decades. In addition to attacks from beyond our borders, there were even worries of being attacked on the roads by thieves and vagrants. Arthur was doing his best to reign that kind of behavior in and he had made great strides, but it did still exist.

But the servants here in the castle's compound had nothing to fear. I stared out the nearest open window and watched the knights from the roundtable and Arthur himself practicing hand-to-hand combat. They were without their armor this morning and many of them were shirtless, their tanned skin already glistening in the early morning heat. All of them were perfectly toned, a testament to their physical prowess. Not a soul in the kingdom wanted to face these knights in battle.

I sought out my soul mate and found him sparring with Arthur's brother, Kay. I smiled. Out of all of the knights, besides Lancelot and Lucan, Kay was probably my favorite.

Good-natured and strong, he stood a head taller than even Lucan. He always had a smile and a good word for everyone, something that I appreciated. Even in a dire or bleak circumstance, Kay attempted to put everyone around him at ease.

Behind them, I saw Gawain, Arthur's nephew, going hand-to-hand with Tristan. It seemed strange to refer to him as Arthur's nephew, because since Arthur's sister was so much older than he was, he and Gawain were the same age. Gawain's younger brother, Gareth, was fighting with the king by the edge of the courtyard lawns.

Arthur, a superior swordsman, was clearly letting the younger knight gain the upper hand and he laughed as he began to hold Gareth at bay.

"Young pup," he laughed, "You must use your legs to anchor you. They're stronger than your arms!"

Gareth growled and lunged again, errantly trying to use his forearms to hold off the King's advances. He wasn't strong enough and Arthur easily toppled him to the ground. Laughing again, Arthur reached a hand down to help him up.

Gareth shook his head good-naturedly as Arthur slapped him on the back. As they rough-housed and joked with the others, I turned my attention back to my mother. I found that she was watching me with a gentle expression.

"They're beautiful, aren't they?" she observed, shifting her gaze to the knights outside. I nodded in agreement.

"But we aren't here to appreciate them, are we?" she asked, leveling her dark gaze at me. I shook my head with a sigh.

"We must find the sword," she needlessly reminded me. "And I think I know where it is. But the problem will be getting it."

I stared at her in confusion. "What do you mean? It's right there." I gestured toward Arthur's hand where Excalibur, his famous sword, gleamed. Guinevere stared at me with raised eyebrows.

"Harmonia, that isn't the sword that he pulled from the stone. Think back."

And at her words, I did remember. The sword from the stone and Excalibur were two separate swords. And the king didn't use the sword that he had pulled from the stone. Merlin had decreed that whoever pulled it from the stone would be the rightful king of Camelot and of course, Arthur had done so… all according to Fate's plan.

He kept that sacred sword safe. Excalibur had been a gift and was the sword that he used in battle and in practice. I sighed.

"So where is it?" I asked. "I don't recall that part."

"I'm not absolutely certain," she admitted, "It's not public knowledge, of course, and he hasn't mentioned it to me. But I believe it to be at his parents' home. He has spoken about a secret room where his father hid hundreds of books to protect them from invaders and looters. I would bet anything that he has hidden the sword there as well. No one would think to look there."

"So we will need to travel to his foster parents' home and ransack it to find the sword?" I raised my eyebrows. "That doesn't seem polite."

My mother rolled her eyes. "You know that no one is there. After his parents died, Arthur kept their home vacant… just another indication that I am correct. He doesn't want to chance anyone disturbing his hidden things."

"Perhaps," I acknowledged, picking up my last piece of bread and chewing on it. In every life, bread had been a comfort food for me. There was no need to change that now.

As I pondered my mother's idea, I felt someone staring at me. I turned, scanning the busy dining hall. In the midst of the clamor surrounding us, a lone figure dressed in dark clothing was sitting a short distance from us, all alone. I would recognize his dark eyes anywhere. He was the stranger from the gardens.

He stared at me, a direct stare that wasn't friendly, but neither was it unfriendly. He lifted his hand in a subtle greeting, then let it drop. He knew that I recognized him. I could see it on his face and somehow, I knew that that fact pleased him.

He wasn't handsome nor was he ugly. He was of average height, his hair light brown. He wasn't remarkable that I could see. I turned to point him out to my mother, but was interrupted by noise and clattering.

The knights were filing in from the courtyard, hungry for breakfast. Servants were already hurrying to fill heaping trenchers for them. Gawain grabbed one and made his way toward the queen and I. But he too was distracted by the stranger.

He stopped short in his tracks, then grinned. Clearly, the stranger wasn't a stranger to him.

"Mordred!" he shouted joyfully. "You've come! At long last!"

He set his plate down beside me and rushed to embrace the man who had seen Guinevere and Lancelot together earlier this morning.

Clapping the man's back, Gawain shouted to Arthur.

"Your highness, my youngest brother has finally arrived! We have found our final knight!"

Arthur smiled in welcome at the same moment that my knees turned weak and my heart seemed to still in my chest.

Mordred. The youngest brother of Gawain and Gareth.
I remembered him now, with sickening clarity. He would be
the downfall of us all.

CHAPTER SIX

Arthur made his way across the crowded hall to greet Mordred, his youngest nephew. Clasping Mordred's hand, he grinned broadly, clearly happy to see him.

"Welcome, young nephew," he greeted him. "I trust your travels here were safe and uneventful? I expected you last week. Did you run into a complication?"

Mordred turned calm eyes toward his king and uncle, quietly deferent but not overly so. My hackles slightly rose, but no one else seemed bothered.

"Nothing that I could not handle, uncle," he replied. "Some minor issues along the road. I am blessed to have inherited your battle prowess and find myself delivered to you safe and sound this day."

"I don't know," Arthur drawled thoughtfully. "You might be too modest to be my relation."

He stroked his chin and everyone around laughed. He could say what he wanted, but Arthur was fairly modest himself. He had single-handedly restored order to Camelot, yet he acted as though he was any other knight from his round table. Of course, part of the knight's code was to practice humility. Arthur expected the same from himself as he did from his knights.

As everyone laughed, I saw that the humor in Mordred's voice didn't reach his eyes and a cold, unsettling feeling formed in my belly. The knowledge that he would eventually topple everything that Arthur worked for put me instantly on edge. And Lancelot and Guinevere had inadvertently given him even more ammunition.

Guinevere rose from her breakfast, crossing to Arthur's side. Although my father was her soul mate, she did harbor true affection for King Arthur. It would be impossible not to. He was a decent man with a good heart. I felt a sense of regret for him. His life should have ended better. I brushed my melancholy aside. I couldn't change it.

Guinevere nodded daintily to Mordred as she clasped Arthur's arm. Out of my periphery, I noticed Lancelot's eyes narrow. I hid a smile before returning my attention to Guinevere.

"Welcome to Camelot, nephew," she murmured. "I trust you will be happy here."

"My lady," Mordred bowed low. As he rose, he kissed her slender hand. "I have seen so many interesting things already. Camelot is full of surprises. I have no doubt that I will enjoy my new home."

My blood ran cold as Mordred appraised my mother and she returned his stare. She knew. I could see on her face that she knew who he was, but no one else would have guessed her anxiety. Her lovely face was as smooth as ever.

"Please let me know if you require anything," she told him politely, before she curtsied quickly to Arthur and returned to my side. As the men talked over their breakfasts, she sank back down next to me.

"What a chilling man," she murmured into my ear. I nodded.

"He is as cold-hearted as they come," I agreed. "I can sense it." Guinevere's eyes glazed over and I knew that she was remembering the last time we had been here.

Even though the Fates were currently imprisoned in Ogygia, they were still firmly in control here in Camelot...because our little skirmish on Calypso's island had not yet happened. Their spells to bind our memories were still active. In my mortal body here, I could remember Heleyne's memories- everything that had happened up until this point in time. Everything in the future was hidden to me.

Although, I was finding that my awakened goddess mind was somehow providing glimpses into the future here that I would not have had otherwise. The glimpses were random and limited, and were both welcome and frustrating.

I somehow knew that Mordred would be the downfall of Arthur, but I couldn't remember exactly how. I could see on Guinevere's face that she was the same.

"Don't fret," I soothed her. "It will all work out."

She nodded.

"I know. I just wish I could remember more." She shook her head sadly.

"Perhaps it is for the best that we cannot," I suggested. "We must leave here without interfering. The Fates might not control us anymore, but I do not know what effects tampering with history would have. We should not take that chance."

"I agree," she replied dejectedly. "But I do not have to like it."

As she spoke, she gazed again at the knights good-naturedly bickering amongst each other as they ate. Arthur was sitting next to Mordred, dipping his bread crust into bacon grease as he chatted with the man who would eventually betray him.

"No," I agreed as I carefully stood and arranged my skirts. "You do not. And neither do I. Come. Let us take a walk or maybe even go for a ride."

That perked her up. She did enjoy horseback riding. She kindly thanked the servant who came to clear our plates and we made our way out of the crowded dining hall onto the winding paths surrounding the castle.

As we strolled, I remembered what these grounds had looked like when Arthur had first assumed the crown. The castle had been crumbling, the grounds overgrown. Within months of winning over the people, Arthur had completely restored the castle and had overhauled the castle grounds to turn them into the beautiful gardens that they were today.

He felt that taking such care of things would restore the will and the confidence of the people. And I had to agree. It had certainly accomplished that. Of course, having a group of strong, well-trained knights on his side hadn't hurt, either.

Pausing briefly, Guinevere bent to pick a dark red rose. She was partial to them and had requested hundreds of rose bushes planted around the palace grounds. Pricking her finger on a thorn, she stuck it in her mouth and sucked on it.

"You know what they say," I reminded her wryly. "Every rose has a—"

"Shut it," she growled playfully. "I might need stitches."

I rolled my eyes. As I did, I thought I saw something move behind me. Turning, there was nothing there. There was only a striped tabby cat from the stables batting a pebble across the path. She chased the tiny stone into the brambles and disappeared.

"What?" Guinevere asked, concern wrinkling her forehead.

"Nothing," I answered. "I thought something was behind us, but it was only a cat."

"Silly girl," she grinned. "Let us ride."

I understood her need to get away from here just for a bit and try to forget what we were facing, so I nodded and we quickly continued to the stables. The old toothless groomsman, Reagan, greeted us. His wiry gray hair stuck out of in tufts beneath his felt hat, making him look slightly deranged. He was a gentle soul, though, and would never hurt a fly.

"Reagan, we wish to have a ride on this beautiful day," Guinevere announced, passing him to stand at the door of her mare's stable. Her horse, Flower, tossed her head as Guinevere stroked her nose. "We shall need our horses saddled."

"Of course, my lady," he bowed quickly, abandoning a saddle that he was oiling in order to saddle our mounts. My own mare, Celine, was a soft buckskin that had just a little more spirit than the average woman would normally care for. I personally preferred it. A horse that was too docile was just plain boring.

We waited while he readied our mares, watching Arthur's black charger paw at the floor in his stall and the barn cats hunt for mice, all the while enjoying the freshly-cut hay smell that surrounded us. The scent, combined with saddle oil, was distinctive to this stable and like scents often do, it triggered memories.

I had spent many stolen hours hidden in the hayloft above us with Lucan. The window upstairs swung open and flooded the loft with sunshine, all while providing a nice private alcove for a pair of lovers. My chest twinged as I remembered those carefree days. I briefly wondered if I would ever be carefree again, but Reagan interrupted my self-pitying thoughts.

"My ladies, your mounts are full of vim and vinegar today," he warned us as he handed us the reins. "They need a good, hard ride. Should I call for escorts?"

Guinevere shook her head. "We won't go far," she assured him. "We just need some fresh air and a good run. We'll be back shortly."

"My lady, are you certain? The King said never to allow you to leave without protection..." Reagan worried, but trailed off when he noticed Guinevere's face. "I'm sorry, your highness," he hastened to add. "I do not mean to second guess you. I will see you when you return."

"Thank you for your concern," she told him with a smile. "But we will be fine." He helped us mount and we rode past him into the sunshine. Once we were safely out of the courtyard and beyond the palace walls, Guinevere turned to me with a mischievous grin.

"I wish I could have told him that we could level an entire army with just one thought, if we had a mind to," she laughed. "The idea that a mere mortal could harm us...that's just funny." She laughed again.

"Mother," I warned, "As far as anyone is concerned, we *are* mere mortals right now, remember?"

"Pftt," she turned up her nose. I sensed the beginning of a minor display of drama and tensed in preparation. "Could a mortal do this?"

She pointed to a nearby rose bush. Every petal on every rose detached from the stem and fluttered into the air, swirling around into a cloud above us before drifting to the ground in the shape of an A. *Aphrodite.*

"Mother," I warned again, then changed tactics. *"Guinevere."*

She sighed. "Fine," she muttered and motioned toward the A. It shifted into a G. One lone petal fell out of formation and she glared at it. It quickly fit itself in with the rest.

"Guinevere," I repeated sharply.

She rolled her eyes at me before finally motioning toward the G one more time. The petals flew into an arrow formation and rushed at my head. I ducked and they sailed over me, separating to once again attach themselves to the stems on the rosebush. They rustled in the gentle breeze as if nothing had ever happened.

I glared at my mother, as I tried to soothe my anxious mare.

"Not funny," I chastised. "What if someone had seen that?"

Guinevere looked around. "Like who?"

I had to admit, she had a point. There was no one around for miles. The green hills rolled on like unfurled velvet for acres and acres on one side, while the sea churned against the craggy shore on the other.

"Like me, perhaps," a low voice suggested and we both spun around in our saddles.

Mordred was leaning against a nearby tree, lightly holding the leather reins to his own horse in his hand.

"You were so absorbed in your theatrics that you didn't hear me approach," he continued. "What are you, pray tell?"

Guinevere spluttered and if the situation wasn't so serious, I would have laughed. She was rendered speechless for the first time in as long as I could remember.

"Sir Mordred!" she exclaimed. "I'm sorry, I didn't realize anyone was near."

"Obviously," he nodded calmly.

"It was just a simple parlor trick," she attempted helplessly. "A stupid thing, really..."

He watched her calmly as she attempted to come up with a plausible explanation. His dark eyes were expressionless. I couldn't tell if he was frightened by her or intrigued.

"A parlor trick?" he asked softly. "I think not, my queen."

He tied his mount to the tree and approached us.

"Are you a witch?" he asked calmly, stopping in front of her. "Does the king know? He does seem sympathetic to witchcraft."

"The king most certainly does not..." Guinevere stopped and stuck out her chin. "I do not owe you an explanation, Sir Mordred," she announced sweetly. "I am the queen. If you have any concerns, you should take them up with my husband, the king."

"Mayhap I will," he replied, his dark eyes glittering. For the first time since he had arrived, I saw an emotion in them. A threat.

Guinevere saw it too and I sighed as I watched her bristle.

It took her two full seconds to leap from her mare and bound to where he was standing. She quickly pinned him to the tree that his horse was tied to, her slender arm braced against his neck. His eyes widened in shock as her goddess strength easily overpowered him.

"You dare threaten me?" she roared with the fury of Aphrodite. I watched her brown eyes cloud and then shift to silver. Mordred's face filled with terror, as any mortal's would. I sighed again.

"No. I meant no threat," he stammered. "Truly, my queen."

"Really?" she purred as she stared into his eyes, her face pushed directly into his. "It seemed like you were."

"No," he practically whimpered. "I apologize, my lady, if it seemed so. I would never threaten you. You are my queen. I mean you only respect and good wishes."

There was a pregnant pause as she assessed him, cocking her head with her arm frozen against his throat. Finally, her expression relaxed.

"That's better," Guinevere murmured calmly, relaxing her hold just a bit. "Look into my eyes, Sir Mordred."

He complied, staring into the silvery depths. I watched in fascination as she hypnotized him with her dulcet voice.

"You will forget that this ever happened," she instructed smoothly. "You were scouting this area and you came across no one. You never saw me, you never saw Heleyne. Do you understand?"

Mordred grew limp against the tree as Guinevere's soothing voice flowed over him like honey. Even the breeze complied with her, dying down to a gentle rustle, the grasses around us bending and swaying soothingly.

"I never saw you, I never saw Heleyne," he repeated in a monotone, staring at her blankly.

"Get on your horse and ride back to the castle," she instructed. "When you see us at dinner tonight, it will be the first time since breakfast that you've laid eyes upon us."

Mordred nodded slowly.

"Yes, my lady."

She released him and stepped away, waiting for him to move. He stayed slumped against the tree, his eyes glazed over.

"Now," she instructed.

He snapped out of it, bobbing his head toward her before dutifully swinging up onto his horse. He galloped away, never looking back.

Guinevere looked at me, shrugging her thin shoulders. As I watched, her breathing returned to normal, the flush disappeared from her cheeks and the silver faded from her eyes, turning once again to deep brown.

"Now, where were we?" she asked conversationally.

CHAPTER SEVEN

After leaving Guinevere in her chambers, I wandered aimlessly through the bustling palace. I didn't know where to begin looking for the sword and to be honest, I was preoccupied with leaving my mother alone. She insisted that she only wanted a nap, that using her goddess strength while in her mortal body had exhausted her. I knew that much was true. But I was anxious that she was secretly going to try and steal time with my father. They just couldn't seem to stay apart.

I sighed. Even though they were very aware of the importance of our quest here and I knew they were completely committed to it, I also knew that my parents sometimes didn't quite grasp the consequences of their actions. As Olympians, they only answered to Zeus and he was currently missing.

As I rounded a corner and turned into a narrow back hall, I heard whispering coming from a room to my right. My curiosity piqued, I poked my head inside the door. It was a small chapel. An altar stood in the front of the room while a massive stone cross leaned against the wall behind it. The cross was so large and heavy, that if it ever tipped over, it would crush anyone in its path.

Heavy wooden benches created rows and the atmosphere was calm and reverent. The room was empty but for one person in the front, kneeling at the foot of the cross. Arthur rested on his knees, his head bowed as he rapidly whispered prayers, a golden crucifix in his large hands.

The light poured in the one window, shining onto his golden curls. Sitting inside that ray of sunshine, he almost seemed angelic. Large and strong, with his sword lying at his side, he appeared as a handsome archangel. His face was creased with worry, however, and his eyes were squeezed tightly closed.

My slippered foot scraped against the stone floor ever so softly as I slipped into the room, but it made enough noise that Arthur heard it. His eyes sprang open and he stood, Excalibur gripped tightly in his hand as he turned.

When he saw me, his expression relaxed and I saw that in addition to worry, he seemed sad as well. His blue eyes were haunted and instantly brought to mind the exchange that I had witnessed between him and Morgan.

It was torturing him. That much was obvious.

"Heleyne," he greeted me quietly. "I thought I was alone."

"Your highness," I curtsied. "You were. I didn't mean to interrupt. I apologize." I started to back out of the room, but he held up his hand.

"No, stay," he requested softly. "I could use some company. Please join me."

His shoulders slumped as he slid into the front pew, as though they held the weight of the world. I instantly felt sorry for him. My nature as the goddess of contentment made me more sensitive to the pain of others than the average person, but anyone could see the agony etched on this man's face. My stomach tightened in response as I padded down the aisle to sit next to him.

"Your highness, are you alright?" I asked softly, staring into his face. He gazed at the ground in front of us, absently fidgeting with the handle of Excalibur. The rubies embedded within the hilt glittered in the light and threw red spots on the wall next to us.

"I am not sure," he admitted finally. "I will be, I'm sure, because I always am. But I am tormented by something. I wish to speak to someone, to draw wise counsel from someone, and yet there is no one that I can turn to with this trouble. You cannot imagine how that feels, can you, Heleyne?"

He turned his pained eyes to me and my heart broke, because they were red and watery. He was in pain and there was nothing I could do for him.

"Your highness... I..." I didn't know what to say. I decided to break rules of etiquette and picked up his hand, squeezing it softly. He allowed the contact and seemed to draw some comfort in it.

"You're bound by oath," he pondered, staring thoughtfully at my face. "I could confide in you and you would be unable to share what I tell you with anyone, not even my wife."

I nodded silently. It was true. Anyone who had confessed fealty to the king was bound by oath.

"But I realize how close you are to my wife," he added, slumping once more, "So, I won't ask you to listen."

Pain emanated from him and I longed to hug him, to try and absorb some of his sorrow so that he didn't have to carry it alone, but that was impossible. For a man of such honor, breaking his marriage vows, even unknowingly, was a great sin. I knew his heart was shattered and I knew that I couldn't alleviate that.

"What of Merlin?" I asked. "Can you not confide in him?"

"No," he answered softly. "I cannot. Not about this."

"Very well," I replied. "Please, your highness. Tell me anything you wish. I can see that you need to unburden. I am loyal to you and I will share what you tell me with no one, not even the queen. I hope that I am able to help you."

"Truly?" he asked, appraising me quietly. "I do not wish to overburden you."

"It will not be a burden," I answered confidently. "I wish to help."

My words opened a dam. For the next half an hour, King Arthur spilled his heart to me on the front pew of the chapel. Tears streaked down his cheeks as he spoke and more than once, I reached up to wipe them away. He was filled with sadness and I could not fix it. But I could hold his hand and listen.

"My soul is sick," he concluded. "I feel physically ill at what I have done and I cannot get over it. It is constantly in my mind, even when I should be thinking of matters of this kingdom. I have wronged my wife so completely. I have gone against nature. I am a monster."

My heart wrenched apart. How could I not comfort such a man? He was good and kind and loyal. For the Moirae to have played with his fate, to have manipulated it into this twisted situation was just wrong. And I found, in this moment, that I couldn't comply with it.

"If you just speak with Guinevere," I suggested softly, "If you just tell her what has happened, I am certain that she will forgive you. This was not your fault. You would never have willingly done such a thing. Guinevere knows your heart, your highness. She loves you."

And she did. My mother had a fondness for him as did everyone else who knew him. It was impossible not to.

"But I cannot," he answered in resignation. "To do so, to admit to Queen Guinevere what has happened, would be to sign my sister's death warrant. No matter what she has done, I do not think I can do that. I cannot burn her at the stake as a witch. I could not live with myself."

"But yet... you cannot live with yourself now, for something that Morgan has done to you?" I raised my eyebrows. "My king, you are good and kind. Everything knows this. Your sister, please forgive me for saying so, is using your own traits against you. She knows that you will not want to harm her, even after she has harmed you."

"Knowing of my sister's manipulative ways does not change my heart," he replied tiredly. "Replacing one wrong with another does not make anything right."

"Might for Right, not Might makes Right, yes?" I quoted his own creed back to him. When he had formed the Roundtable, he decreed to live by a set of rules and one of them was to use his strength for the public, not to use it against them. It was a belief that he lived by.

"Yes," he sighed. "Might for Right."

I fell silent, considering his situation. If he admitted what had happened to the queen, if it passed from his lips to her ears, then he would be forced to punish Morgan. There had to be some way to ease his pain, some way that didn't add to it. I wracked my brain.

"What if...." I began, but trailed off.

"Yes?" he asked, his face so hopeful that I couldn't resist it.

"What if I am the one who spoke to the queen on your behalf?" I suggested weakly. To interfere in such a way was not bright. I knew it even as I spoke, but I couldn't help it. He was shouldering so much pain already.

"I could explain what has happened and tell her that you long to discuss it with her, but that you cannot. I am sure she will understand and forgive you, and your heart will be unburdened. Your marriage will be cleansed of lies."

"You would do that?" he asked, his voice wavering. "Truly?"

I nodded, swallowing hard. "Yes. Truly. If the queen understands and forgives you, then Morgan cannot extort her will from you. She will have no leverage."

He grinned broadly and leaned over to engulf me in a tight bear hug. I could scarcely breathe, my face smashed against his broad chest. He finally released me and I took a big breath, filling my lungs with much needed oxygen. He laughed and I had to smile in reaction. The king looked better already.

I wish I could say the same for myself. My birthmark, which had been bewitched to ache whenever I did something that the Fates did not approve of, was throbbing mercilessly. I tried to ignore it, gripping it tightly with my other hand.

"I'm glad to be of help," I murmured meekly.

"Of help?" King Arthur asked with raised eyebrows. "You have saved me. Make no mistake about that. You have saved me, Heleyne, and I am indebted to you."

"No," I shook my head. "You are not."

"We'll agree to disagree then," he nodded, "Although... I'm the king so I am always right." He threw his head back and laughed, the joyful sound ringing through the chapel. "I owe you and if you should ever need me, I will assist you. I always repay my debts."

I was just murmuring a thank you when Merlin strolled in.

His black eyes cut me like a knife and I flinched. I could see in them that he knew what I had just done, how I had just agreed to interfere on the king's behalf. To interfere in this now was to interfere with Fate, something I had never purposely done. His face was stark and severe as he entered the chapel.

"Your highness?" Merlin called down the aisle. "Your attention is required in the Knight's Hall. Could you accompany me?"

Although he spoke to Arthur, his gaze was pinned on me, holding me tightly to the wooden pew. The king didn't notice. Arthur couldn't see the way my shoulders were restrained against my will. I felt my backbone grind into the hard seat and I gritted my teeth. Merlin was punishing me for my interference and I was sure that he would have more to say on the matter later.

"Of course, Merlin," Arthur answered, rising from the pew. "I'd be happy to. What is the issue?" Turning to me, he lifted my hand and kissed it with royal lips.

"Lady Heleyne, I thank you for your ear and for your kind words and assistance. I look forward to your company at dinner."

With that, he strode down the aisle to join Merlin and they discussed Merlin's issue as they disappeared down the hall.

I will speak to you later.

Merlin's voice appeared in my mind just as clearly as if he was standing next to me and he released his hold on me. I stretched my shoulders as I shook my head, willing myself not to answer him in kind. As a mortal, I had never been able to return his silent messages to me. I couldn't do it now as much as I might want to offer a sharp retort. Instead, I gathered my heavy skirts and retreated from the chapel to find my mother.

She wasn't going to be happy when she discovered that I had interfered. She didn't want to see Arthur suffer either, but as she had already pointed out, interfering would cause changes and we had no idea what the consequences of that might be. I sighed.

I descended the stairs and walked quietly past the Hall of Knights. As I passed the cavernous room, I glanced inside. Merlin had his back to me as he stared out an open window. The cool breeze blew through and pushed my hair off of my forehead.

The knights were seated around the large roundtable. All of them leaned on the famed table wearing serious expressions.

"The Saxons have dispatched mercenaries?" Arthur demanded incredulously. "How do we know that it wasn't the Romans?"

"We do not," Merlin admitted from the window. "It could be either."

"What is important, your highness, is that we are being invaded by pervasive tactics. We have not faced this before," Lucan spoke from across the table. "These intruders are acting as marauders from our own country, seeking to instigate riots among our own by pillaging and murdering to undermine the king's competence in protecting the people. It must stop."

There were murmurings of agreement and I watched Lucan for a moment from the doorway. He was intense and focused as he assessed the threat to his country. His sense of honor was outweighed by nothing else. He was created to be a warrior.

He glanced up and saw me watching and dipped his head in acknowledgement before he returned his attention to his peers. The simple act of his gaze meeting mine caused my heart to thrill. And with that, I remembered my purpose here, my sole purpose in life. I had to save him.

Walking on, my thoughts were consumed with Lucan as I made my way to Guinevere's quarters. I was determined to save him and I lived for seeing him. Whatever it took, I would find the sword. But first, I had to speak to Guinevere about Arthur.

Opening her door quietly, I was immediately assailed by the scent of roses. Glancing around inside, I had to laugh. There were hundreds of them here. As usual, my mother had gone overboard. I inhaled the thick scent as I made my way to her massive, curtained bed.

And I froze in my tracks. Standing next to her bed, clad in a dark gown and veil, was Morgan le Fey. *Eris.* She was standing motionlessly over my mother, watching her as she slept. My heart practically stopped beating and I gasped.

At the sound, Morgan's head snapped around and she all but snarled. Before I could even react, she was gone from the room in a flash, disappearing in a blur of black through the doorway. Like a streak, I followed her, watching the spot of color slip around the corner of the hall. Using goddess speed, I followed her.

My pursuit landed me at the doorway of a room in the bottom of the castle. At the very dregs, next to the dungeon, the door I was facing was plain and wooden, free of any embellishment whatsoever. Breathing quickly, I pushed the door open.

Morgan faced me from across the room, standing over a shimmering mirror.

"What are you?" she hissed. "You are not human."

"Why were you in the queen's rooms?" I answered her question with a question. "You have no right to be there."

"I can feel that there is something different about you," she replied. "And something different about her, as well. I will determine what it is."

"You cannot enter the queen's chambers for a whim," I sniffed. "That is not your right, even as the king's sister. And certainly not when he is so disgusted with you."

She clenched her jaw and I could tell that I struck a nerve. She had used her position as Arthur's sister to her advantage on more than one occasion. It annoyed her that it was a perilous position now, even though it was of her own doing.

"And *you*," she snarled. "You act so pious and wise, yet I have seen that you will be undone by a child. A child! All that you are, everything that you value, will rest in the hands of a child. Yet you speak to me as though I am the fool."

My heart slammed in my chest. I would be undone by a child? What the hell was she talking about? I focused on her malicious face, pushing the troubling thoughts away. I could think on them later.

"I did not speak to you as a fool," I corrected. "You are not a fool. You are evil, but not a fool. However, your back is to a wall now. You have boxed yourself in with your brother. What will you do?"

"I do not answer to you," she hissed and she disappeared, leaving me alone in the damp darkness of the musty room.

I stood for a moment, gathering my thoughts, before I looked around. Thick books of magic with weathered covers were scattered about, a large mirror was lying in the center of the room surrounded by a circle of ash. Clearly, this was her hideaway where she dabbled in witchcraft. Or, at least, she thought it was witchcraft. What she didn't know was that any supernatural ability that she had was a direct result of her true identity.

As I ruffled through parchments filled with writing, I came across one that stilled the breath on my lips. An entire parchment was full of notes about mythology and Morgan's theories about Zeus' sword. Her thoughts about his sword would not have been alarming but for one minor detail. No mortal was aware of its existence.

CHAPTER EIGHT

Harmonia, where are you?

I heard my mother's question in my head, her voice strangely sharp. Instantly, I imagined myself with her and within a second, I appeared at her side in her bedchambers.

"You shouldn't do that," she observed, her long hair pulled over her shoulder. "What if someone walked in at just the right moment and saw you?"

"I know, I know," I dismissed the concern, "But you sounded upset and we have an issue."

"Of course we do," she sighed. "We have many issues."

"This one is pressing," I replied and I told her of what I had found.

"Now I'm upset," she responded, rising to stare out her window. She tapped her finger furiously along the bricks of the sill, the rapid cadence a clear indication of her agitation.

"And that's not all," I continued.

"Of course not," she muttered. "What else?"

"I… er… interfered."

"Interfered?" she turned with a raised eyebrow severely. "What do you mean, interfered? With what?"

"We should sit," I suggested and led her to her bed. Sinking into the softness, I shared what had happened with Arthur in the chapel. When I was finished, her face was a rigid mask of frustration.

"Harmonia!" she exclaimed in her best mother's voice. "We've talked about this. We don't know what will happen. You cannot interfere."

"But I already did," I pointed out. "It's already done."

"You can just turn right around and go back to him and tell him that you changed your mind. That you do not want to interfere." My mother's face was stubborn and set mulishly.

"Tell the king that I've changed my mind?" I asked doubtfully. "I don't think that would go over so well. And mother, you should have seen him. I couldn't bear it. He's in so much pain. And once I said that I would help, that I would talk to you, he lit up like a light. I can't crush him. I can't."

Guinevere sighed. "You've got a soft heart, daughter. I suppose I shall have to do what you cannot."

"What do you mean?" I asked suspiciously.

"Well, you told him that you would speak to me. And you have. So now, it's in my hands, isn't it? I'll just have to take a hard line with him. I simply won't forgive him."

I gasped.

"Mother, don't," I pleaded. "Truly, if you could just see him, you would know why I feel so strongly. He's a good man and he doesn't deserve any of this. He's crushed from what he thinks that he has done- only it wasn't his fault. None of it is."

My mother's face clouded over and she opened her mouth to speak, but a commotion from outside caught our attention and we hurried to her windows to look. The castle's giant gates were open and two wooden wagons slowly rolled in, pulled by tired mules and surrounded by raggedly dressed pheasants. They were in an uproar and we tried to see what the fuss was about.

I watched their dirty faces and found them full of emotion...anger, sadness, outrage. Their clothing was in tatters, most of them barefoot, all of them filthy- spattered with mud. I held my breath in trepidation as the wagons drew closer, creaking past the main hall entrance and coming to a slow stop directly beneath Guinevere's windows.

Bodies were piled in the wagons. They were bloodied and mutilated, old and young. My eyes were frozen on the body of a child, his tiny arm dangling from the foot of the wagon bed, his small fingers open and blue. I sucked in my breath and my gaze met Guinevere's.

"Holy Mary..." I trailed off.

My mother's face was severe, her mouth pressed into a hard line. "They need us," she said simply.

We hurried from her rooms and rushed to the foyer, where Arthur was just exiting to meet them. We followed closely behind.

"What will you do?" a peasant woman cried, reaching out to touch Arthur's velvet cloak. "How will you protect us now?"

A thin man to her left met my gaze before he looked to the king. "They murder us in our beds, while you dine on fancy meals and dress in fancy clothing. You are no different from your father at all. You only want to seem like it."

The man dropped to his knees and cried next to the wagon, reaching out in his grief to grasp the tiny dead boy's hand. I assumed that he was the boy's father and I felt a tear drip down my cheek.

"By the gods," Guinevere breathed softly. "This is evil."

"This is what you don't wish to change," I pointed out quietly. "The will of the Fates. They do this for their own entertainment."

My mother fell silent and I turned to a nearby servant. "I need clothing. Gather others and bring us as much clean clothing as you can find. And ready any empty guest room that is available here in the castle."

The servant girl looked to Guinevere, who nodded.

"Do it," she murmured.

The girl turned on her heel and ran for the interior of the castle as I turned my attention back to the bedraggled group of strangers. Women were weeping, men were shouting. It was utter chaos.

Amid the confusion, Arthur stepped on the ledge of the nearby gardens, making him a few heads taller than everyone else.

"Countrymen," he shouted. "Listen to me!" It took him a few more attempts before the crowd quieted enough to hear him.

"Do you think this will go unpunished?" he called. "Do you think that Arthur Pendragon will allow his subjects to be beaten and killed within the very borders of his country? I will not. I vow to you today that by my very own blood, I will protect you. My knights will ride to their last breaths to protect you. Camelot will be strong and we will be victorious. We *will* avenge this!"

At his last word, the crowd erupted into cheers, so loud that they made my ears ring. Arthur looked fierce and determined as he assessed his people.

"We will protect you," he added. "You have my word."

He stepped from the ledge and strode into the castle, motioning his knights to follow. They fell into line and disappeared into the castle with him, Lucan included. I watched their broad shoulders vanish down the hallway before I returned my attention to the peasants in front of me.

Joining Guinevere, I helped the servants hand out fresh clothing and linens. Seeing a small group of children standing apart from the rest, I switched directions and headed toward them, a stack of clean linen in my arms.

Kneeling next to them, I asked, "Where are your parents? Were they killed?"

The child in front nodded solemnly, dried tears streaked on her dirty cheeks. Four or five smaller children crowded behind her, each too shy to meet my gaze.

"Come with me, then," I instructed. "Let us clean you up. You will sleep here at the castle for now."

I grasped the girl's hand and ushered the others to a well standing not too far away. Drawing up a bucket of water, I dipped a soft linen into it and wiped at the girl's face.

"Everything will be okay," I assured her. "I know it doesn't feel like it, but it will."

The girl nodded silently and let me attend to her before she stepped to the side and sat down. I motioned for the next child to step forward and when she did, I startled.

It was Raquel.

Long blondish hair straggled down her back and bright blue eyes peeked from behind the dirt on her face. She was the young girl who the Fates had brought from Calypso's island and left on Olympus to instruct us where to meet them. Why was she here now?

Gesturing her forward, I grasped her skinny arm.

"What is your name, child?" I asked casually as I washed her face.

"Gwendolyn," she whispered. Her pink lips had the same curve to them that Raquel's did. She was the same child. My heart started skipping beats. What did this mean?

"Gwendolyn," I repeated. "What a beautiful name! And so very close to our own queen's name. That makes you special," I added. "Queen Guinevere will be so honored to hear of this."

"She will?" the child asked shyly as she fidgeted nervously with her foot.

"Of course she will," I assured her. "In fact, stay with me and I'll introduce you to her in a few minutes. Would you like that?"

The child looked at me in wonder. I knew she had probably heard all about the new king and his beautiful queen from her parents. To meet them now was beyond anything she'd ever imagined.

"Were your parents killed, as well?" I asked gently.

"No," she answered. "I do not have parents. I've been an orphan since birth."

"I'm sorry for that," I replied softly. "But we will find a place for you here. And you will belong."

She smiled, a beatific smile that didn't quite make it to her eyes.

"Thank you, my lady," she murmured, dipping her head. Above her, I sought out my mother from across the courtyard. Catching my gaze, she made her way to my side.

"Heleyne, are you almost finished here?" she asked, drawing next to me curiously. "We should ready the extra bedrooms inside."

"Of course, your highness," I answered. "But first, I'd like for you to meet Gwendolyn." I patted the little girl's back and she stepped forward. My mother's eyes widened when she saw her.

She knelt, grasping the child's hand.

"Hello there, little one," she murmured, staring into the child's heart-shaped face. "I like your name."

"Your lady told me you would," Gwendolyn answered shyly. "It's nice to meet you, your highness."

"And it is so very nice to meet you," Guinevere answered. "Would you like to stay here with us for awhile?"

Gwendolyn nodded. "Yes, please," she replied. "I don't have anywhere else to go." She dropped her head in shame and I lifted her chin with a finger, forcing her to meet my stare.

"That is not your fault, young one," I assured her. "You will be taken care of here. Are you hungry?"

She nodded, as did the other children around her. I motioned for a nearby house servant.

"Please get these children something to eat in the kitchens," I requested the girl. "And then show them to a clean guestroom. I'll check on them later."

She nodded and hurried away with them, leaving me to stare at my mother in bewilderment.

"What is going on?" I asked. "Why is she here? And in the same exact body as in the Spiritlands? There is not one thing different about her but her name. Her hair, her eyes, her voice is the same. And in the Spiritlands, I found her in a pile of rubble, also. Here, she came to us with a group of orphans. There must be a correlation, but what? You know that it must mean something. The Fates are using her for a reason."

My mother nodded, her eyes absent as she thought. "I know not," she finally admitted. "I will consult with your father when next I see him. Perhaps he can remember something that we can't."

"Have you seen him this afternoon?" I asked suspiciously, but her eyes widened innocently.

"No, of course not," she replied quickly. Almost too quickly. "I've been in my rooms and the knights have been with Arthur. There has not been an opportunity. But I will make sure that I do tonight."

"Just use care," I cautioned her, my eyes suddenly drawn to Mordred, who was standing at a window above us. He was watching me with glittering eyes and an almost menacing expression before he turned away. "I feel as though we are being watched."

"Well, we probably are," she shrugged her shoulders. "You knew that this life wasn't easy when you came here, Heleyne."

I nodded wordlessly, watching the hungry peasants assemble around the servants carrying large platters of warm bread for them. Dirty fingers reached to snag pieces of the fragrant prizes as the servants pushed through the teeming crowds.

There were so many of them, all homeless now, some of them orphans, some of them parents who had lost their children. Grief was everywhere around me and there was nothing I could do about it. And it wouldn't be so hard to bear if it was simply a random act of violence. But the fact that Fate orchestrated all of these horrible things simply to entertain themselves while they ruled in Zeus' rightful place made my blood boil.

"I feel weary of this," my mother whispered as we sank onto a nearby bench. "All of the pain and suffering. It wears on me."

I reached over and grasped her hand.

"You read my mind," I agreed. "It is horrible. Life is not always fair, but with the Fates involved, it is never fair. And that is an atrocity."

She nodded her head in agreement, watching the melee in front of us as peasants scrambled for food and items of clothing. We tucked our feet underneath of us so that we wouldn't get stepped on in the chaos.

We sat that way for a good while before Arthur once again emerged from a side doorway of the castle. Scanning the crowd, he quickly found us and the sea of people parted to let him pass as he made his way to our side.

Bowing low, he took Guinevere's hand from mine and kissed it gently, his blue eyes seeking out hers. In his, hesitation and fear lingered and I knew he was afraid that she had not forgiven him. I watched anxiously, waiting to see what she would do. Unable to bear the thought of Arthur's pain, I almost squeezed my eyes shut so that I didn't have to witness it.

But before I could, my mother stood and pressed her lips to Arthur's. In surprise, his hands clasped at her back and then he pulled her into him for a deeper kiss. As the crowds around us cheered, I met my father's dark stare from across the courtyard. He turned abruptly and stalked from the commons. I felt a twinge of guilt.

It must be hard for him to be here, to watch his beloved married to someone else. Once again, we were stuck in a parody of the Fates' choosing.

Guinevere finally pulled away, her cheeks flushed. Arthur kept her clenched to his side as he turned to face the crowd.

"In Camelot," he shouted. "There is always hope. And when there is hope, anything is possible!"

The crowd cheered once more and I clapped with them, happy to see the joy that was shining on so many faces. Arthur was truly a charismatic man, someone whose very presence could excite crowds, someone who people innately trusted.

But as I stood in appreciation of the atmosphere, a wave of nausea washed over me. Intense heat flushed my cheeks and the courtyard began to spin. The sea of faces and noises blended into one another and before I knew it, I was on the ground with my cheek resting in the dirt.

CHAPTER NINE

My mother raced to my side and knelt next to me.

"Heleyne," she uttered as she rubbed my back. "What is it?"

I tried to open my eyes but every time I did, dizziness threatened to make me vomit. I moaned just slightly, but enough to cause my mother to panic.

"Heleyne! Are you in pain?" She looked into the crowd. "Someone send for the medicine woman!"

Before anyone could move, Lucan pushed through the throngs of people and lifted me into his arms. I gazed up at his handsome face for just a moment before I squeezed my eyes shut against the dizzying nausea.

"When you find her, send her to Heleyne's rooms," he instructed my mother over his shoulder. His long steps made short work of the courtyard and before I knew it, we were entering the cool darkness of the castle.

Once out of the sun, I opened my eyes. Lucan was staring at me worriedly as he carried me down the halls toward my bedchambers.

"Are you alright?" he asked anxiously. "You're very pale."

"I'm fine," I answered, although in truth, I felt horribly weak. My hands were shaking and I didn't know why. "I feel better now. I think maybe I got too hot in the sun."

He glared down at me. "You shouldn't tax yourself so much, woman."

"But it is nice to be rescued by a knight in shining armor," I quipped lightly.

Unfamiliar with the phrase, he scowled at me. "I'm not wearing armor."

Kicking my heavy door open, he crossed my bedchambers in four long steps and laid me gently down on the softness of my bed. Pacing back to my window, his boots clicking on the stone floor, he looked outside.

"I don't see the old woman," he muttered impatiently, pacing back. Sitting on the edge of my bed next to me, he grasped my hand.

"How do you feel?" He was so anxious.

I had to smile. Lucan was perfectly at home on the battlefield, but one sign of sickness or tears and he fell to pieces, at least when it came to me. He had always been that way. I reached up and brushed his dark hair away from his forehead and he leaned into my hand.

"I'm much better now, my love," I answered softly. "I'm happy to be with you."

He grinned a cocky grin, one that was still laced with concern. "Heleyne, there are better ways than this to spend time with me, I assure you."

I laughed and he laughed with me, his voice husky and rich. I felt like I could take a bath in the sound.

A soft knock resounded on my open door and I glanced up. An old medicine woman creeped into the room, her back hunched and her face concealed by a heavy black hood. She trudged across the room, my mother following on her heels.

With one arm, she motioned Lucan to move away from me. He stood, but I could feel his reluctance as he lingered close by.

"Move," she hissed to him. "I do not want you here."

Lucan's head jerked up and he glared at her. "Old woman, I would like to see you make me leave," he thundered. "This woman will be my wife. I will know what ails her."

The old woman turned to him, her fragile back humped grotesquely. "And you shall. You shall know when I tell you. But you will wait in the hall. Go."

The look on Lucan's face was priceless because for once, he was speechless. The woman, who was barely four feet tall, certainly knew no fear. I spoke up.

"My love, I will be fine. We'll send for you when she is finished. Trust me, I feel better already."

He glared once more at the old woman before bending to brush a kiss on my forehead.

"I'll be waiting," he assured me. I nodded and watched him stride across the room and disappear into the hall.

After he left, the old woman slowly turned to me and I gasped.

She was the same woman who had brought Cleopatra and I the deadly snakes in ancient Alexandria. Was nothing ever what it appeared? What kind of tricks were the Fates playing? Was everything simply a game to them? I turned to my mother and found the same startled look. She recognized the woman, too.

The old woman's face was ancient, thick wrinkles lining it. She was the oldest living person that I'd ever seen. Her curled fingernails rasped against my clothing as she began to undo my buttons.

"What are you doing?" I asked, pushing her hands away. "I feel much better now. I can keep my clothing on."

"Heleyne," my mother interrupted. "Let her examine you. You really don't look well."

I glared at my mother for a moment before allowing the old woman to continue her examination. Nausea threatened to overwhelm me with every breath that I took. There was definitely something wrong with me.

The old crone took several minutes unbuttoning my gown and then she shoved it out of her way as she felt along my back, her calloused fingers trailing along my skin. Goosebumps formed wherever she touched. Her fingers drifted along my spine, up to my neck, back down to my sides.

"Lie back," she instructed gruffly.

"Your bedside manner could use some work," I grumbled as I complied with her request. My head rested in my pillows and I tried to imagine that I was anywhere other than here as the old woman's probing hands explored every inch and orifice of my body. I kept my eyes glued to the stone ceiling as she pushed my legs apart, my thoughts firmly with Lucan.

Finally, she raised her head and stood upright.

"You will be fine," she announced matter-of-factly. "You are with child."

"With child?" My jaw dropped open. "You must be joking. You're mistaken- that's impossible."

I could feel my mother's eyes frozen on me as I stared at the old woman. She nodded once again, her leathery face impassive.

"I do not make mistakes," she confirmed. "You are with child. I am certain."

She drew a handful of sage from her robes and laid it on my nightstand.

"Burn this in your rooms," she instructed. "It will ward away evil spirits. Some spirits try to take the unborn."

She turned and trudged toward the doorway. I was in too much shock to reply. My hands automatically flew to my stomach, which was still completely flat. In wonder, I flattened my hand out, gripping at my belly. Could it be true?

"I don't know," my mother answered my silent question, crossing to sit next to me. "I don't see how."

"I've always thought that I was barren," I continued, still palming my belly. "The Fates always told me that Keepers couldn't have children. But obviously, I'm not a Keeper, so..."

"So, maybe it is true," Guinevere acknowledged. "The Fates cannot control you as a goddess. They could only control your mortal form."

"But I'm in mortal form now," I replied in confusion. "So I don't understand how it could be."

My mother was already shaking her head. "Your body here is mortal, but you've already been awakened as a goddess. As long as you are aware of it, you are a goddess no matter what body you are in."

"But how can this body be pregnant?" I wondered, still completely in awe at the idea. I would be a mother?

My mother chewed at her lip. "If I had to guess, I would say that you brought the pregnancy with you. It makes sense. You and Cadmus were together in the Spiritlands, were you not?"

My cheeks flared as I nodded. This simply wasn't something that anyone wanted to discuss with her mother. But she was right. We had been together in the Spiritlands... beginning in Eris' bathroom and then again in Zeus' palace. It truly did make a pregnancy possible.

"Then, I do think that you brought the pregnancy with you," she concluded. "Your mortal body isn't pregnant, your true body is. Once you leave this place, Heleyne will no longer be pregnant. You will take it with you to the Spiritlands."

"As confusing as that sounds, that makes sense," I agreed. "Which means that we will need to rush our business here. Heleyne is not meant to be pregnant. We cannot have her body begin to show."

"I agree," my mother said. "But we should rush anyway. We absolutely must find that sword and soon. Where have you looked?"

"I've managed to search in several halls and the rotunda in the right wing. As of yet, there is no sign of it." I sighed. "Where have you looked?"

"In Arthur's rooms. It was not there," she admitted. I sighed again.

"Do not fret," she instructed. "We will find it." She sank onto the bed next to me, pulling me into a hug.

"Congratulations, daughter," she beamed. "We shall have to restore the palace nursery in Olympus. I cannot wait to spoil this child. Although, I must say, I'm too young to be a grandmother."

"You'll be the most beautiful grandmother on the face of the planet. You are ageless," I assured her. "But this brings with it so many complications. We are in Camelot, Cadmus is trapped in the Wastelands, the future of the Spiritlands is uncertain…"

"The future is not uncertain," Guinevere stated firmly. "We will save the future. We have no choice. For now, all you can do is use caution and protect the child that you carry. All will work out, daughter."

She smiled Aphrodite's smile at me and I couldn't help but return it. I was pregnant. It was a miracle. I was filled with such a feeling of wonder that I could hardly contain it. My mother beamed at me once more as she stood.

"I'll leave you to rest," she said as she walked toward the door. "And I'll send Lucan in. I'm sure he's beside himself right now. Do not tell him," she cautioned.

"I won't," I answered as I nestled into the softness of my pillows. Lucan was beside me in one minute flat, sliding up next to me, wrapping me inside his strong arms.

"The queen said that you are fine?" he inquired, nuzzling the back of my neck. "That you simply got too warm. Is that correct?"

No, I'm carrying your child, I wanted to say. But of course, I did not.

"Yes, my sweet. It is just as I thought. These skirts do get warm in the heat. I feel so much better now," I assured him. Ecstatic, exuberant and joyful, to be exact.

"Do not scare me like that again," he instructed, pulling me closer into the warmth of his hard chest and I inhaled his masculine scent. He smelled like the outdoors.

"I won't," I promised as my heavy eyelids closed. I was so weary. It felt as though every cell in my body was tired and I knew a nap would do me good.

But even still, sleep wouldn't come to me. All I could think of was how much I wanted to share my miraculous news with Cadmus. He was going to be a father and he didn't even know.

As I snuggled deeper into Lucan's arms the strangeness of my current situation hit me. I was here with my husband, but he was in another body and didn't know who and what we were. I was pregnant with his baby, but I couldn't tell him because he had impregnated me from his god form, not his mortal form. And I couldn't tell him in his true form because his true form was trapped by the Fates in some godforsaken wastelands. If I hadn't known it before, I would certainly know it now. The Fates were cruel, cruel beings.

At long last, my eyes grew too heavy and I felt myself drift into slumber. And almost immediately, I found myself standing face to face with my husband amid swirling white wind.

"You're pregnant?" he asked incredulously.

Unfortunately, although amazement and joy was inflected in his tone, I knew he didn't feel it in his heart. He wanted to, but he couldn't muster it up in this horrible place.

I nodded. "How did you know?"

He shook his weary head. Lines were etched on his face now, lines that hadn't been there before. The wastelands were hard on him and I ached to take him from here. I had never felt so helpless.

"I do not know. Every once in awhile, something just occurs to me. I don't know how. It is just dropped into my mind."

I thought on that for a moment as the wind whipped my skirts around me. Was it possible that he was inadvertently gleaning information through his life as Lucan?

He paused and ran his gaze up and down my length. "By the gods," he breathed. "You've traveled time again, haven't you?"

I nodded. "Yes," I answered. "It was necessary. I think Zeus' sword is in Camelot. We've returned there to find it so that I can save you."

He examined my clothing once again, his eyes widening.

"You're in Camelot?" he asked in shock. "Do you remember how dangerous it is there for you? I have no wish for you to be there. You must return to the Spiritlands. We'll find some other way to get to the sword."

"There is no other way, my love," I shook my head. "We'll find it, I'll return, then I'll save you."

"And then you'll spend all of eternity reminding me of that?" he raised his eyebrow humorlessly. Again, it was something that he would normally say in jest, but it was apparent that all laughter was gone from his heart.

"I'm going to be a father," he marveled as his jaw clenched. "I can't believe it, Harmonia. What a blessing!"

"Yes," I whispered. "And I cannot wait to get you back home so that we can truly celebrate it in the happiness that it deserves."

"I'm sorry, wife," he murmured, pulling me to him. "I will be happy. I promise it. This place sucks every emotion out of me, I cannot help it. But I do love you. And I will love our child. It will be the most loved child in the history of the world."

Tears streamed down my cheeks, soaking the front of his tunic, as sadness for what I was now missing overwhelmed me.

"I know, Cadmus. Ours will be the luckiest child in the world."

He glanced down at me. "So, you've managed a way to be with me, even though I am trapped here. You've always been wily, wife."

I smiled against his chest. "It wasn't my purpose, but I will admit that being with you as you are Lucan is a comfort to me right now. I miss you so much, Cadmus. But I am trying my best to save you. We will beat them, I promise you that."

He nodded silently, his large hand stroking my back.

"I know," he answered. "I have faith in you, Harmonia. But leave here now. You don't belong here, especially now. Protect our child."

And I was awake.

Lucan was stroking my back in the same way as Cadmus had been a moment ago, his long fingers splayed across my hip identically. And although it was comforting, it wasn't quite the same. Somehow, even though I had loved Lucan with every ounce of my heart, Cadmus was who owned it.

A large part of Cadmus existed in every mortal life that he had lived, but he wasn't truly himself except for when he was Cadmus, because only then was he truly aware of who he was. It was more pressing than ever that I get him back - not only for me, but for our baby. I curled my hand against our unborn child protectively and closed my eyes once more.

CHAPTER TEN

The castle herald woke me from my nap with a bugle and his grating shout.

"Hear ye, hear ye! The royal tournament will continue as planned for this eve. A feast will ensue after." I could tell that he passed beneath my window and then continued onward, because his annoying voice grew more distant. "Hear ye, hear ye!..."

I rolled to my side and found Lucan's eyes open. His arm was under my shoulders.

"King Arthur is still having the joust" I asked. "Even after the massacre of the peasants?"

Lucan shrugged. "I believe he probably wants life to continue as normal, as much as possible. Why should we allow the Saxons to change what we do?"

"Or the Romans?" I added. "It could be either, from what I heard."

"True," he acknowledged. "Although, my lady, this is something that you do not need to concern yourself with. That is my job as your man. I won't allow harm to come to you."

At times like this, I did truly miss Cadmus. Cadmus, in his true form, knew very well that I was perfectly equal to him in every way. In our earlier mortal lives, not so much. I swallowed my annoyance and smiled cockily.

"Yes, Lucan. You are correct. I should sit by the fire and embroider something."

He grinned. "You're such a cheeky one, Heleyne. Anyway, it is too hot to sit by a fire. You'll have to sit outdoors in the shade or in the queen's bower." I swung around and punched him on the arm and he laughed.

"You're not meek enough by half," he observed. "But I love you to distraction."

"As I love you," I answered softly, stroking his bulging muscle where I had just punched him. "But do not become distracted this day, Lucan. Not at the joust."

He rolled his eyes as he stood.

"Must you think so little of me?" he looked toward the ceiling in mock despair. "Do you think me so unskilled? I will win tonight, my lady. For you. Shall I carry your favors?"

"Of course," I replied lightly, rising from the bed to choose a red scarf from my armoire. "We'll tie this around your arm."

He took it and bowed low. "I will have my squire see to it," he said obediently with a grin. "And I will win the tournament for you."

"Only for me?" I asked doubtfully. "Not for the fame and glory?"

He shook his head. "Only for you. I will hand your scarf back to you as a champion."

I shook my head with a smile as he dipped to kiss me and walked from my rooms. I took one moment to straighten my disheveled hair and set out to find my mother.

It wasn't hard. She was overseeing the servants who were setting up the seats for the joust. I crossed the field to the side of the castle, treading across the wildflowers and grass that led to the jousting arena.

One side of the arena backed up to the cliffs that the castle itself was situated on. I stood on the edge for a moment, looking down. The ocean crashed below me, magnificent and strong, with sandy beaches unfurling for miles on each side. Amid the call of the seagulls and the smell of sea salt, I closed my eyes with the sun on my face.

The baby was rapidly stealing my energy and I would swear that I could fall asleep in this standing position if I stayed still too long. Shaking the weariness from my eyes, I turned to meet my mother.

On either side of the arena, wooden tiered benches were arranged for the crowds. On the far end, there was a box filled with seats and a bright green canopy overhead snapping in the wind. Arthur's green crest hung in front, just below the seat that he would sit in, if he didn't participate. However, there was seldom a joust in which he did not participate. His seat, like normal, would sit empty today.

Next to him, was Guinevere's seat and my own, as well as several other chairs for visiting dignitaries and any noblemen of the kingdom who were in attendance. From this vantage point, we had a perfect view of the tournament. Any time a knight crashed into the dust, his lance splintered, we would see it perfectly. And to be honest, right now I just didn't have the stomach for it. Men from this era so loved blood and sport.

"I wish that Arthur would cancel this today," Guinevere muttered as she straightened the chairs that we would sit in. Turning, she took a vase of flowers from a servant girl and placed them on a pedestal in the corner of the gallery box.

I didn't know why she bothered. The smell of the roses would not come close to overpowering the strong scents of horses, manure, dust and blood that would fill this stadium in a little while.

"We do not have time for this," she grumbled to me. She looked at the servant girl who was patiently waiting for further orders.

"You may go," she nodded kindly to the girl. The girl turned and walked down the steps leading to the gallery and Guinevere looked back to me.

"Well? What say you? We do not have time for this."

"What would you like me to say, mother?" I stared at her in exasperation. Aphrodite had such a tendency to work herself up into a frenzy and expected that her agitation would spill to everyone around her. And sometimes it did. But not today.

"Yes, we have more important things to do. But we cannot help that right this moment. Our absence from this joust would be missed. We will resume our search for the sword tonight after this tournament. I wish to search this castle from top to bottom before we hunt away from here. It makes no sense otherwise."

Guinevere finished tying a bow on the banister in front of me and stopped, pausing to survey the area in front of us. The arena was empty and quiet, the bleachers free of people. She sighed.

"I know you are right," she murmured. "I'm sorry for adding to your stress. I know you must be anxious already. You are correct. We will thoroughly search the palace grounds before we search elsewhere."

As we descended the wooden steps from the gallery tower, I tossed my hair out of my face and as I did, I caught sight of Morgan sitting in the far seats of the arena, back in a darkened corner. Hunched with her, his head to hers, was Mordred. My blood turned cold as I stopped moving. My mother ran into my back, and I felt her follow my gaze, then heard her sharp intake of breath.

They were talking animatedly; Morgan was throwing her hands around wildly and finally Mordred stood, glaring down at her in agitation before barking something at her. He stood still for a moment and then stalked down the wooden walkway and across the field back to the palace.

Morgan watched him go and then she turned her head, meeting my gaze. Her eyes were dark and stormy and froze into mine. I felt as though I would ignite from the heat emanating from her glare. Finally, she turned her head and leaped to her feet, flouncing away in the opposite direction. Her dark cloak swirled around her and I watched her disappear into the tunnels under the arena.

"What was the about?" my mother whispered in my ear.

"That is a good question," I answered. "The two of them together is a worrisome combination." She nodded in agreement, but we didn't have time left to continue the conversation. People from nearby villages were beginning to arrive for the evening's joust.

I sighed as I settled into my chair, watching the stands fill up with peasants, farmers and noblemen. To our right, Reagan and his stable boys led out the knights' horses. All of them were decorated festively, with masks and ribbons while banners draped from their backs. Pageantry was a large part of jousting. Every action was steeped in tradition, going back hundreds of years. It was a celebration of honor and chivalry and Arthur thought that it was a good reminder to the people of what he stood for.

Arthur himself was laughing with Sir Tristan a few yards from us. They were both already wearing their armor, each of them holding their helmets in their hands as they talked. Tristan's sandy blonde hair curled around his shoulders, his brown eyes warm as they twinkled with jest. He was typically a quiet man, very thoughtful in everything that he did. But he was very loyal to the king and just as deadly as anyone else seated on the roundtable.

Arthur slapped Tristan on the back, his hand clanging against the metal, before he turned and walked quickly for Guinevere. Bounding easily up the steps, mindless of the heavy armor, he knelt in front of his queen.

"My lady, may I wear your favors?"

His cornflower blue eyes beseeched her and I saw just a glimmer of insecurity in them. He was afraid to trust that she had truly forgiven him. It spoke to a soft place in my heart and I smiled at him.

Guinevere laughed, a soft tinkling sound. "Of course, husband." From her skirts, she withdrew a satin kerchief, tucking it into the front plate of his armor. "Wear it here, by your heart," she instructed. "My love will protect you, your highness."

My heart swelled with pride for my mother. She did so carry out the part that she was meant to play here. And even though her true heart belonged to my father, she treated Arthur with the love and respect that he deserved. She truly earned the title of queen.

He grinned in response, bending to kiss her hand.

"I shall win for you," he told her solemnly. I couldn't help but pipe up.

"Then you shall have to best Lucan, my king. He has sworn to win for me, as well." We all laughed, Arthur hardest of all, before he rose to his feet and bowed slightly at his waist. "Well, Lucan is certainly a worthy adversary. I will do my best."

He straightened and grinned at us both.

"Ladies," he said. "I will return in a few moments." He turned and began walking noisily down the walkway. "As a victor, Heleyne!" he called over his shoulder.

I couldn't help but laugh as I watched him join the rest of his knights. They were all congregating around their horses as their squires finished final preparations.

This joust would only be between themselves. They did host tournaments when they invited other challengers from throughout the land. Those competitions could turn deadly. But with the current state of the country, Arthur couldn't risk losing any of his highly trained knights to a simple jousting loss. He needed them on the battlefield. These tournaments now were for fun and sport. A simple exhibition only, one meant to restore the morale of the people and to provide sheer entertainment.

I watched Lucan's squire tie my red scarf around his bicep over the metal of his armor. Lucan looked up at me, catching my eye and winked before he dropped the visor of his helmet.

Instead of taking the stairs back up to the gallery, Arthur leaped onto the ledge in front of us, balancing precariously as he addressed the crowd. Clad as he was in heavy armor, it was a sheer testament to his athletic prowess.

"Countrymen!" he shouted. "We all know that we face challenges ahead from enemies from other lands. They come here, to our own land, to challenge us. But today… today we will put this aside and in this exhibition, my knights will show you the caliber of the men protecting you. You will see that your country is in good hands. Let the games begin!"

Bugles sounded and he leaped once more to the ground. Flags fluttered from the corners of the stands and people laughed merrily, all willing to forget the current dire situation of the country in exchange for one joyous evening.

First up, were Arthur and Tristan. As they faced each other from opposite ends of the arena, the court herald leaned from a small box protruding from the bleachers at the midpoint. When the king participated, the herald acted as an official in his stead and ruled the winners. The herald lifted his arm, a flowing black scarf in his hand, then dropped it.

At his signal, King Arthur and Tristan rode for his each other, their lances held tightly under one arm as their horses' hooves thundered in the dirt. As they drew closer, anticipation built and then they met in the middle. Their horses did not swerve and they each lifted their lance, their faces invisible from behind their visors.

Arthur made the first contact, striking Tristan sideways on his chest, squarely across his chest plate. Arthur's weapon knocked Tristan from his seat, causing him to sprawl headfirst into the dust.

Arthur spun his horse to face first the crowd, with his arms raised in victory, then to Guinevere. He dipped his head and then straightened again before sliding from his horse. Walking to Tristan, he helped him from the dirt. They both flipped up their helmets and chatted as they walked from the arena. Their squires scrambled to retrieve their weapons and horses, clearing the area for the next dual.

Gawain and Gareth competed next, two brothers pitted against one another in fun. They each winked to the crowd before facing off, causing the eligible ladies in the crowd to giggle and watch the men with interest. Both of them were eligible bachelors, and they both incited much interest from the females in the kingdom.

After Gawain good-naturedly prevailed over his brother, they shoved each other out of the arena, much to the crowd's delight. Sir Bedivere and Sir Kay followed them with Kay as the winner. Gaheris and Bors de Ganis were next.

As they faced off, Guinevere whispered to me.

"How are you feeling? Are you okay in this heat?"

I reached over and squeezed her hand. "I'm fine, your highness. The breeze is nice, though, is it not?"

The ocean breeze blew in from the sea, breaking up the horse and dust smells. Without that, the smell around the arena could become stifling, particularly to a newly pregnant woman. It seemed that all smells were becoming more potent to me now. I could even smell the sweat from the horses from here.

"Oh, look!" Guinevere nudged me. "Lucan's turn!"

My eyes shot to the arena to seek out my soulmate. He was poised, tense and ready, waiting for the scarf to fall. It dropped, fluttering in the wind, and he and Sir Percivale went head to head, their horses' massive hindquarters digging into the dirt as they ran.

Lucan raised his lance and deftly knocked Percivale from his seat. The crowd erupted into cheers and Lucan rode directly to my feet, taking off his helmet.

"For you, my lady!" he called. I blushed and blew him a kiss. The crowd roared once more and Guinevere laughed, while Lucan retreated to help his brother-in-arms out of the dirt.

I glanced toward the end of the arena to find Mordred tensed and at attention, waiting for the signal to begin. As the newest knight, it was his turn to face Lancelot, the king's champion. Even though this was simply an exhibition, tradition must be adhered to.

Mordred's eyes were trained with razor sharp precision on my father as he dropped his visor and something about his stare put me instantly on edge. Everyone else was jovial and light-hearted. But Mordred was icy and tense. The hackles rose on my neck as the black scarf dropped in the wind.

They tore off for each other and as Lancelot raised his lance to knock Mordred from his horse in a sweeping motion,

Mordred raised his lance as a javelin. While Lancelot's arm was raised, Mordred impaled my father beneath his arm, in one of the few spots where armor was vulnerable.

The crowd gasped in unison and Guinevere jumped from her seat, her hands covering her mouth as Lancelot tumbled from his saddle.

"Mother, don't," I warned as she hurried for the stairs. She ignored me and rushed into the arena. We were closer than anyone else, so we were able to get there more quickly than Arthur. He too hurried for his champion's side, but Guinevere reached him first.

Easing off his helmet, she murmured, "Are you alright?"

"Of course," he nodded slowly. "It is but a scratch."

Pushing in beside my mother, I lifted his arm and examined the wound. Mordred's lance was embedded a few inches beneath Lancelot's right arm. I swallowed hard. A mortal could bleed to death from such an injury.

Mordred had yet to dismount, instead sitting above us, the evening sun casting his shadow over where Lancelot lay.

"This was an exhibition!" I snapped up at him. "What were you thinking?"

His face was meant to be sympathetic, I'm sure, but to me he seemed impassive as he apologized to the King.

"Your highness, I apologize. I meant no serious injury. It was a slip of the lance. I have only the utmost respect for your champion and I beg your forgiveness, uncle."

Arthur clenched his jaw and remained silent as he knelt beside Guinevere. Gripping the lance firmly, he wrenched it from my father's side. Lancelot groaned and blood gushed from the wound. I quickly took off my cloak and wadded it up against the injury, hoping to staunch the blood.

Arthur called to the knights, "Come- bring your shields. We must carry him inside."

The knights quickly brought their shields and laid four of them on the ground in a line. They transferred my father onto the makeshift gurney and then carefully carried him toward the castle with Mordred straggling behind them. Arthur turned to his squire.

"Find the medicine woman," he instructed. "And hurry."

The boy took off running as Arthur studied his wife. She still sat in the dust, her skirts tangled around her legs, next to a pool of Lancelot's blood. Her hands were visibly shaking, her face pale.

"Are you alright, my queen?" Arthur asked in concern, reaching down to help her stand. "Your concern for my champion is admirable. You have a very kind heart."

She nodded and allowed him to pull her into an embrace, and she laid her head onto his shoulder. He patted her back gently for a moment, before stepping back, gazing down at her. His blue eyes were full of emotion.

"I must see to Lancelot," he said. "But I will see you at dinner." He looked to me. "Can you see her to her chambers, Heleyne?" I nodded.

He strode quickly from the arena, but as he retreated, I noticed the strangest look on his face and my heart stilled for a moment. It seemed that perhaps my mother had given herself away.

CHAPTER ELEVEN

"By all that is holy!" my father thundered.

I smiled under my breath. I could hear him all the way down the stone hall. The medicine woman had already attended to him by cleansing and dressing his wound before she decreed that he would live.

But he was pissed.

Apparently, my father wasn't enjoying the limitations of mortals, in particular the slow healing process. I knocked lightly on his door and found him propped in his bed, while a page tried to help him into a clean tunic.

"I do not need a shirt!" he yelled in agitation. The boy shrank away.

"But sir, you must be dressed. Particularly in the company of a lady…" he trailed off at the look on my father's face.

"I do not give a rat's front teeth about decorum right now," my father enunciated clearly and loudly. "I have a hole in my side! Have you not noticed?"

I smiled and motioned for the boy to leave.

"I can assist the kind knight," I told him gently. "Why don't you bring something for him to eat?"

The page more than happily took his exit while Lancelot scowled. "I am not hungry, either," he informed me, his expression dark and sulking.

I stepped closer and rounded the bed, my skirts trailing behind me with a rustle.

"Um, you do know that you are the god of war, right?" I asked with a raised eyebrow. My father stared at me for a moment before exploding into laughter, holding his side as he did.

"Maybe," he acknowledged finally. "But the god of war should not be reduced to weak mortal form. This is unacceptable…and painful."

I patted his leg. "Perhaps," I agreed. "But you've done it for thousands of years and have been none the worse for it."

"None the worse?" he asked incredulously. "Have you not noticed the hole in my side?"

"So we're back to that, are we?" I grinned. "You'll be fine. My worry now is not your injury. It is Mordred. He tried to kill you and make it look like an accident. What did he call it? A 'slip of the lance'?"

Lancelot instantly sobered. "Yes. He did. And he will not live to do it again."

"Father," I cautioned. "You know that you may not seek retribution. Not right now. His death isn't meant for you."

My father's glare was dark enough to eclipse the sun. He didn't intimidate me. I shrugged. "You know it's true."

He sighed heavily, stretching one leg gingerly in front of him. "Maybe," he acknowledged and then changed the subject. "How is your mother? Is she worried sick?"

He actually sounded pleased by the prospect. I rolled my eyes.

"She was," I offered. "But then she remembered who you are and how strong you are and she realized that you would be fine. She did send me to check on you, though."

He settled back into his pillows with a satisfied expression, reaching over to pick up an apple from his nightstand.

"You're both treading a thin line," I told seriously, as he took a bite. "Arthur noticed that mother was the first to your side in the arena. I saw it on his face."

For once, my father took what I said seriously and I watched him ponder it.

"You know," he said thoughtfully. "I never thought I would say this, but I actually like your mother's husband. He's a good man."

"Yes, he is," I agreed. "And you will both break his heart."

"Perhaps," he replied. "But I won't enjoy it."

"Like that matters," I muttered beneath my breath. "Okay. I've checked on you. You're fine, but for a foul mood. I will report back to mother and then I will continue to search for the sword. I only wish to find it and leave here. We can leave Camelot behind us and never think of it again. What say you?"

"I say that you'd better be jesting," Arthur said as he stepped into the room. My gaze flew to his face and he studied me curiously. "Leave Camelot? You can't be serious."

I nodded. "Of course, your highness. I was simply telling Sir Lancelot that with his luck of late, he might be better served to ride away from Camelot and never look back. But of course I was simply jesting. Where would the Roundtable be without your champion?"

Arthur nodded and I curtsied.

"I'll take my leave, your highness. I simply wished to check on Sir Lancelot's injuries. He appears to be back to himself."

Arthur nodded and turned his attention back to his knight and I slipped from the door, pausing to lean against it as I gathered my thoughts. I had almost given us away to Arthur. I really would have to be more careful.

The hall was empty, but for me. This section of the castle contained bedrooms, all of which were usually empty during the day. The queen's bower was here, a quiet place where she was supposed to sew and do womanly things, although I didn't think that Guinevere had used it even once since we'd been here.

Down the hall from the bower was the solar, the long room used for entertainment for the royal family. Court jesters and musicians performed for the family in the evening hours, after they had retired from dinner and before bed. It too was empty now.

A thought occurred to me and I ducked inside. Heavy chests lined the far wall. They were intricately carved from oak, each standing three feet tall. Kneeling next to one, I removed the velvet table-runner from the top and unlatched the clasp, lifting the heavy lid.

Thick tapestries were folded inside. I rifled through them, feeling for anything metal within their depths. When I got to the bottom, I even checked to see if the chest had a false bottom. It did not. I sighed and began refolding the tapestries, wishing to leave it as I had found it.

"Are you looking for something?"

Merlin's quiet voice came from behind me and I spun around. He was standing with his arms folded, silently observing me. I had no idea how long he had been watching me.

"Yes," I answered calmly. "A table-runner. And lucky for me, I have found several."

He remained impassive as I finished folding the soft material and closed the lid of the chest.

"Is there anything else I can help you find?" he asked me, his black eyes glittering.

"No," I replied. "There is nothing that you could find that I cannot, Merlin. I am as familiar with this castle as you are."

"Really?" he asked, his lip curling with amusement. "And have you ever been *here*?"

Instantly, we were standing in the bowels of the castle…in the oubliette, the most feared and treacherous room of the castle. Situated in the dungeons, it was a small dark room where prisoners were sometimes left to die. It was devoid entirely of light, for there were no windows. Thankfully for me, Merlin held a torch in his hand.

The smell was overwhelming and sickening and as I glanced around me, with my hand over my mouth, I saw why. A partially decomposed prisoner was in the corner, flies buzzing around him as squirming white maggots covered open wounds.

His eyes were open and glassy, while a few maggots even clung to the yellowed, crusty corners. As I watched one crawl from his slack mouth, nausea welled up and I couldn't control it. I bent over and vomited onto the floor. The smell of this place coupled with the sight of the maggots was simply too much to bear. My pregnant mortal body couldn't handle it.

Once I had emptied my stomach, I stood once more, wiping my mouth with my arm and facing Merlin.

"Why did you bring me here?" I asked. "I don't wish to be here."

"No, of course you don't," he agreed. "No one does."

He held his torch above our head, illuminating the ceiling.

"Look above us, Heleyne. See that small hatch? That is how prisoners are lowered in here, with a rope. And that is how food and water is occasionally brought in as well, until that time which they simply decide not to do it anymore and the prisoner is left to starve. Or die from his wounds, whichever happens first."

"Does Arthur know of this place?" I asked as I looked around once more. Condensation dripped in the corners, dropping annoyingly to the floor. Listening to that long enough would be enough to make someone crazy.

Merlin shrugged. "Maybe, maybe not. His father certainly used it often enough. Although Arthur may not personally authorize its use. I believe Kay is the one, as the castle steward, who oversees it now."

I froze in disbelief, thinking of Kay's friendly smile.

"Kay knows of this place?" I breathed.

Merlin scoffed at me. "Heleyne, these men are knights. They are not lambs. They do what they do for the better of the kingdom. What do you think they should do with murderers? Slap them on the hands?"

"No," I muttered, unconsciously rubbing my stomach. "I suppose not. It just surprised me. Kay is so gentle."

"Yes," Merlin agreed. "He can be. And he can also be deadly. That is a good lesson for you, keeper."

"And that is?" I raised an eyebrow.

"People are not always what they seem. These knights are chivalrous and brave, but they all possess the ability to be deadly and cruel if need be. Even your beloved Lucan."

I hated that thought, but I knew it was the truth. It was the nature of a warrior.

"Why are we here?" I asked again.

"I just wanted you to see it," he said. "I wanted to remind you of that very thing. That is all."

"Then, if we are finished here, I'd like to return upstairs."

He nodded and we were once again standing in the solar and I took a deep breath of fresh air.

"I'll leave you to your hunting," he told me as he walked toward the door. "I hope you find what you are looking for."

After he left, I followed him to the door, making sure that he was indeed gone. The halls were empty, so I rushed back to the remaining chests, and hunted through the last three quickly.

There was nothing but banquet linens, tapestries and silverware. I slumped to the floor with a sigh. No sword. Where in this kingdom was it? My very existence depended on finding it.

"Heleyne, I've been searching for you," Guinevere called as she padded softly through the door. "Merlin told me that I could find you in here. What are you doing? He said you were searching for something."

Her arched eyebrow raised even further.

"I've searched through this castle, mother," I murmured. "I've even just been to the oubliette. There is nothing here." My shoulders slumped. "We've got to find it." I heard the desperation in my voice and I hated it, but I couldn't rid myself of it.

My mother rubbed my shoulder comfortingly.

"We'll find it, daughter," she replied softly. "Do not stress yourself so. You must try to remain calm for your child."

My hand fluttered to my belly. I had forgotten for a moment that a baby rested within me. I hadn't yet felt it move, so it was easy to forget, but for the occasional bouts of nausea.

"Where shall we look next?" I asked. "How will we travel to Arthur's parents' land without someone wondering why?"

"We'll sort it out," she replied absently, staring out the window as she spoke. I followed her gaze to find Arthur and his knights in the courtyard. Lancelot had just limped in to join them.

"What a fool!" Guinevere muttered. "Can he not just recognize that he is but a mortal right now?"

I watched him for a moment, observing how even though he limped, he moved just a little too fluidly for someone who had just sustained a near mortal wound.

"He has healed himself," I announced quietly. "Look at him. He moves about too easily. He healed his wound. Perhaps not fully, but enough that it no longer causes him pain."

My mother shook her head. "What a cheat," she grinned as she glanced back at me. "What, daughter? You cannot help but admit his gall."

"It's not gall, it is stupidity," I answered. "What if Arthur sends the old woman to check on his wound? And she will find it healed. Then what?"

"We'll worry about that when the time comes," she answered without concern. "I'm sure it will not be an issue. Instead of worrying yourself over such things, let us think about where next to search for the sword. That is enough to worry about."

I nodded and absently watched my father interact with the knights. He glowered at Mordred, but did not say anything to the knight who had tried to kill him. I had to give him credit for that. I knew that he wanted to run him through with his sword.

"Time passes us by," I whispered, palming my slowly growing belly. "And with every second, my love remains in the wastelands, cold and alone. Please... let us just find the sword and save him. In doing so, we will save us all."

Guinevere turned her gaze from the courtyard and agreed.

CHAPTER TWELVE

The small brook feeding the courtyard bubbled soothingly, the sunlight reflecting off of the surface in multi-colored prisms. I sat on a nearby stone bench, alone with my thoughts, as Guinevere attended to the evening's menu with the cook and Lucan hunted with the rest of the knights.

Around me, everything was quiet. The late-afternoon sun bathed the gardens in warm light, long ago drying off the light rain from the morning. The white roses next to me allowed their sweet scent to waft into the breeze and I inhaled it deeply. For the first time in quite a while, I was alone. And while I enjoyed it, the silence allowed the magnitude of everything that had happened lately to catch up with me.

How was everything going to work out? I couldn't help but wonder. I had been marked as the Chosen One, but I didn't feel very significant. I hadn't even seen my own father's injury coming. The strange thing was that my wrist hadn't hurt even once since it happened. Apparently, it was something that the Fates had planned.

I turned my wrist over and examined my birthmark. The bird-like shape had lost its vibrant red coloring since I had left the Spiritlands and had once again faded to a natural light brown.

The Chosen One. I had the power to command the phoenix, something I had only recently remembered. Something that had saved my skin not too long ago. As the goddess of harmony and contentment, I was naturally inclined to fix issues, to smooth over problems.

But this… this was one massive problem. And I just wasn't sure that I was strong enough or skilled enough to make it work. And I was in uncharted territory. I subconsciously palmed my belly again. I had to face the unknown while I protected a baby.

"What are you thinking?"

Merlin was suddenly beside me and I flinched from surprise, yanking my hand from my stomach.

No matter what body he resided in here, he was always going to be Ahmose to me. And no matter how many times he did it, I would never enjoy his sudden appearances. I scowled at him and replied with my customary answer.

"Can you please stop doing that?"

He smiled with crooked teeth, but quickly sobered.

"I cannot read your mind, dear Heleyne, and that is very strange. You'll have to tell me what you are thinking." He patted my arm with his wrinkled hand nonchalantly, but I could see on his face that it was very troubling to him.

Apparently, my goddess mind blocked his thoughts, something that he wasn't used to. When I was mortal, before my goddess tendencies had been awakened, he had been able to use my mind as a playground. If I wasn't careful, I would give myself away. I quickly focused on the inadvertent protective wall surrounding my mind. I consciously let the wall fall away, exposing it to Merlin's inquisitive poking.

He smiled.

"Ah, there we are. How strange. That has never happened before."

I made a conscious effort to quickly hide certain thoughts from him, tucking them back behind the invisible wall, giving him access only to the most inane and unimportant things. He wrinkled his brow.

"Strange," he murmured, searching my face quizzically.

I kept my expression blank. I felt badly for him, I knew he did his best to protect me from the Fates, but in the end, he was still their pawn. They controlled him and I well knew it.

"What do you think of Mordred?" I asked randomly. Merlin had no idea that I already knew Mordred's purpose here. I watched him try to form an answer, something that I couldn't help but find amusing.

"I know not," he shook his head. "I doubt his intentions are good, but we cannot help that, can we? We do what we do and they do what they do. It is out of our control."

He shrugged his bony shoulders and I could swear that I caught a whiff of the thick incensy scent that had always accompanied him in Alexandria, but before I could even process that, the smell was gone.

I found myself wondering how much he truly did know, how much the Fates allowed him to understand. From what I knew of them, they probably kept his knowledge limited. He was simply their puppet, something thankfully I no longer was.

"I have a feeling that you are right," I agreed. "Something doesn't feel right with him. He gives me chills. And I think he purposely tried to kill Lancelot." I ran my hands up and down my arms automatically, even though he was nowhere near.

Merlin glanced at me before staring into the distance. "I need to find Arthur. Are you alright here?"

"Of course," I assured him. "I was just...taking a break. I needed some alone time."

He nodded in understanding. "Alright then, Keeper. Enjoy your quiet time. I'll see you at dinner."

He was gone before I could even answer and I shook my head. I gathered up my skirts and started to get up myself when a bird landed beside me. I startled again, sinking back into my seat.

A falcon, large and beautiful, sat beside me with rich golden-brown feathers. Falcons were used for sport here, for hunting games and for sending messages. But there was something different about this one, about the way it was watching me.

It cocked its head and examined me, lifting a sharply taloned foot.

A rolled missive landed in my lap. I glanced at the bird before picking up the little rolled paper. It was as still as stone while it waited for my response, its fathomless black eye unblinking.

Unrolling the message, I found the feminine scrawl of Lachesis, the middle sister of the Fates.

By the waterfall at midnight.

Strange. Lachesis typically appeared to me whenever she felt like it. She didn't orchestrate meeting times. She simply felt that I would adapt to whenever she chose to visit. This was very unusual and it put me quickly on edge. Did she know about the child? Surely not. She wouldn't wait to confront me.

The falcon flapped its wings one time, demanding my attention. It cocked its head.

"Alright," I murmured. "You may tell her I will be there." As if I had another choice. To defy the Fates would tip our hand.

The falcon dipped its head in acknowledgement and flew away. The message in my hand burst into flame and I jumped away from it. It burned with a bright blue fire for a scant second, before absolutely nothing, not even ashes, remained.

Still annoyed, I gathered fresh roses to put in a vase in my room and then gathered a few more for Guinevere before heading inside to ready for dinner.

* * *

King Arthur had taken too much ale. He stood at the head of the main table, laughing and attempting to speak to the dining crowd. He started to speak, slurred his words, laughed and started over. Everyone in the room laughed with him. He very seldom was carefree and seeing him so tonight was enjoyable, even to me.

"My countrymesh…men. Countrymen," he corrected. Grabbing onto the ledge of the table, he steadied himself before continuing. "We've worked so hard thish, er, these past few months and we deserve a break this eve. I'm having bottles of fine wine brought around to your tables. Pleash. Please, enjoy with my compliments and gratitude. With you, Camelot is becoming one of the greatest cities to be found."

He raised his glass, sloshing dark red wine onto the white linens gracing the table as he lost his balance. He grinned sheepishly at Guinevere, who smiled gently at him, patting his arm and murmuring into his ear. Craning my goddess ears, I focused in and listened.

"My love, you may want to ease up on the wine this eve. I think you've had enough."

I raised my eyebrow. My mother was exhibiting caution? This was unusual.

King Arthur laughed and answered. It was clear that he thought he was whispering, but I definitely did not need to employ goddess hearing in order to understand him. He shouted loudly enough for the closest four tables to hear.

"Wife, let us make merry. Then let us make love. Let ush make love this eve. It's been too long." The crowd tittered and my mother blushed delicately.

"There's a reason for that, you besotted fool," Lancelot growled softly from my left.

Only my mother and I heard him, since he spoke so low, but both of us shot him warning glances. Ares' jealousy was legendary. It would not do for it to raise its ugly head while he was Lancelot.

He leveled his dark gaze at me, gripping the table so tightly that his knuckles turned white. I heard a crack and saw a piece of the thick wood table break off in his hand. I glared at him even more sharply and he let go of the table, tossing the broken piece onto the floor. Thankfully, no one noticed.

"Your highness," he called, making his way through the chairs until he reached Arthur's side. "I have some important matters to discuss with you. Might you have a free moment?"

Arthur nodded seriously before lurching to a shaky standing position.

"Of course, my champion. But then I must go. I musht attend to my wife."

I felt sorry for him- only because he would never normally discuss Guinevere in public in such an indelicate way. He was honorable to the extreme. His behavior tonight would leave him humiliated tomorrow. Down the table from him, I found Morgan smirking into her goblet and I briefly wondered if she had put something in his wine. It really was unlike him to become so sotted.

Lancelot discreetly allowed Arthur to lean onto his arm, helping him walk from the hall with dignity and I felt a deep sense of gratitude to my father. It was kind of him to help Arthur in such a way. Mordred thoughtfully watched them retreat, silently eating as he observed his drunken king and uncle.

They disappeared into the hall and I returned my attention to my dinner. At the end of the room, the jester was already singing a ballad about the intoxicated king of Camelot. I shook my head and picked at my roasted pheasant. I had never been a big pheasant lover. But when in Rome... I picked up my fork.

Just at the tines reached my lips, the warning bugles sounded the alarm outside and everyone froze for a second, before jumping to their feet, silverware clattering all around me. Everyone began clamoring every which way before Lucan leaped from my side and shouted above the din.

"Everyone, listen! Calmly walk back to your quarters. *Calmly.* We will have the matter well in hand soon."

Since he had absolutely no idea why the alarm was being sounded, his statement was pretty brazen. But everyone listened. They stopped running and quickly filed out of the hall, presumably to return to the safety of their chambers.

"You too," Lucan instructed in my ear, before brushing a quick kiss on my lips. "I'll return soon. Stay safe in your chambers. Bar the door behind you."

He crossed to where the other knights were congregating at the head table and waited for Arthur and Lancelot before they quickly exited to the outdoors.

"Stay safe," I murmured after them to the empty room.

Guinevere and I silently sat staring at each other. Even Merlin was gone, a fact that was slightly troubling. Usually in situations like these, he found his way to my side in an effort to keep me in check. But there was no trace of him now.

"We should go," Guinevere suggested. "You know that we can help them if need be."

"And you know that every time we do, we risk being discovered. We cannot," I answered wearily.

"Of course we can," she insisted. "We are goddesses. We are not bound by mortal law or reason. We can do as we wish."

"Mother," I gritted my teeth. "We cannot. We must leave this place as we found it. No one can know what we truly are."

"And no one shall."

And she was gone. I glanced around the room quickly, but just as I feared, she was nowhere to be found. A weight dropped in my belly. She was following them, I knew it. I sighed heavily. Why, oh why, did my mother have to sometimes be such a loose cannon? I pushed away from the table and willed myself into the courtyard. Within a couple of seconds, I reappeared by the stream.

I quickly hid behind the nearest tree, the violet shadows of night concealing me. I was thankful that my dress was mossy green. It blended easily into the darkness.

From across the way, torches burned brightly as the knights prepared to ride from the castle compound. Horses stomped and snorted, and the metallic clang of armor resounded throughout the compound as the knights made their preparations. The lookouts shouted down from high on the wall.

"Twenty riders, Sir Kay!" one shouted to Arthur's brother. "Make that twenty-five. They are armed and armored."

"Arthur!" Kay roared from his mount. "Can you ride?"

"He'll be fine!" Lancelot answered. "He'll stay by my side."

I knew that if Arthur didn't ride, it would be whispered about throughout the countryside and once again, I said a silent thank you to my father for saving his hide.

The knights were finally readied and someone opened the gates for them to ride out. They filed out, their horses' hooves pounding like thunder as they galloped through the wall. And at their tail-end, I found my mother, riding Flower and concealed by a dark cloak with a hood. I groaned.

I quickly visualized myself on Flower's back in similar attire and I was immediately there, grasping Guinevere's slender waist and whispering into her ear.

"Mother, what are you doing?" I hissed. "This is unacceptable."

She laughed quietly. "We do what we must, daughter. Would you have me leave your father unprotected, while he cares for Arthur? Someone needs to watch his flank."

"He has a fleet of skilled knights to do that," I replied wryly. "He has no need for you."

"Bah!" she tossed her head. "Mortals. I should entrust his well-being to mortals?"

I didn't bother to answer. I knew it was of no use. The only thing I could do now was hang on and hopefully reign her in when the time came.

The horses kicked up dust as the knights rode hard to intercept the intruders. I had no wish to be discovered, so I pulled my hood tighter around my face, shivering as I did. I had no idea who the strangers were or what they wanted, but if they were armed and armored, they meant us harm.

The moon shone high and brightly in the sky, adding light to the flickering torches that the squires were carrying for their knights. The atmosphere was charged and tense as we raced toward the unknown threat. I knew that I could interfere at any time, that I could use any number of my goddess strengths to intercede, but I also knew in my heart that I could not. This must unfold as it naturally would and I would have to allow it.

I only hoped my mother had that much sense.

As we drew near, the horses slowed to a trot and then to a walk as the knights separated into a battle formation. Since my mother and I were concealed by hoods, no one had noticed our presence as of yet. It was simply assumed that we were squires in the surrounding confusion.

Since we were in the back, we couldn't see what was happening. But we heard grumblings of discord and then the battle bugle was sounded. My heart raced in my chest at an inhuman rate. Lucan was at the front with my father and Arthur. And though he was a skilled warrior, I couldn't help but feel twinges of worry for him.

The metallic clash of swords echoed throughout the still night and I clutched my mother's sides tightly as I tried to control myself. I desperately wanted to use immortal talents to fix this situation, to keep Lucan safe…but I could not. I gritted my teeth and waited.

And then my mother jumped from our horse. As she ran in a streak toward the front, her hood fell away and her long chestnut hair streamed behind her.

The squires in the back froze before they came to their senses and tried to grab her. They were too slow. She slipped like a lithe shadow in between the foot soldiers until she reached the front. In desperation, I followed closely on her heels, trying to reach her before Arthur or Lucan saw her.

But I was too late.

Just as Guinevere burst from the confines of the crowd of soldiers, Lucan and Arthur spotted her at the same time as one of the deadly marauders they were fighting. The stranger appraised her with glittering eyes before he reared back and lunged with his long lance. Guinevere wasn't even watching-she only had eyes for my father. She didn't see the danger she was in.

Before I could reach my mother to yank her back, a young squire leaped in front of her, protecting her from the flash of the sharp blade. It glittered in the moonlight before it sank deeply into his thin chest, plunging through his back before he crumpled onto the dirt.

My mother gasped and whirled around as I dropped to my knees beside the squire. Blood was gurgling from his pink, boyish lips and his breathing was already raspy. Around me, the fighting continued, but I didn't pay attention. I could only concentrate on this one boy.

His life, so very fragile, was slipping away. I could feel it, the vibrant cords of it were fraying, disappearing into the night in a very tangible way. And all I could do was to stop myself from grasping at them, to keep from trying to pull him back to me.

"Please, tell my mum that I love her," he begged me and then he coughed, crimson blood trickling from the corner of his mouth. "Please."

His face was as pale as his blonde hair, growing paler by the moment as he lost more and more blood from his wound. As it was, his blood was pooling around my knees. I could feel the wet warmth against my legs, soaking my heavy skirts. And my resolve broke. I knew I had to help him. He was so young... too young.

"Tell her yourself," I instructed him, placing my hands firmly on his wound. "Watch me, boy. You're fine. Keep your eyes on my face."

I pushed against his wound with my hands, all the while feeling my bloodstone throb against my ribcage under my dress. As I poked against the gaping, bloody hole in his body,

I felt the crushed bones inside jab sharply against my fingers. He cringed and so did I.

I opened my mind, allowing goddess energy to flow into the boy, into the jagged wound. I blocked out any thought other than channeling my energy into him. The strange portal opened, just as it had when I had saved Hasani in Alexandria and I held it open, waiting for this boy to heal enough to live.

I could feel stares beating down on me from all around, so I prayed that he would heal quickly. And thankfully, he did. His youth and purity helped him heal quicker than an older man would and within a few minutes, I was able to pull away. His wound was still there, but it was no longer deadly.

As I sat back, I found my strength depleted and that I barely had the energy to stand. My shoulders slumped and my mother came quickly to my aid, pulling me to her side and letting me lean into her.

"And you told *me* to behave," she chided into my ear.

If I had the strength, I would have spit out a sharp retort, reminding her that we were only in this situation because of her. But I did not. From the corner of my eye, I saw the boy sit up to gain his bearings and then stand. He kept his hands pressed against his wound, but he was doing well. He would live.

His blood covered me in huge splotches and I allowed my eyes flutter closed. It no longer mattered to me who we were fighting. I didn't have the strength to care. I didn't even have the strength to be angry with myself for interfering. I sagged into Guinevere, attempting to stay upright.

And then suddenly Lucan was with me, scooping me into his strong arms. I nestled against his armored chest as he strode quickly with me toward safety, away from the fighting, away from the nervous and probing stares of the witnesses.

Guinevere followed closely behind. I could hear her cloak as it dragged on the ground behind her.

When the noise from the battle had faded away, I opened my eyes. We were in a small clearing not too far away. It was quiet here and Lucan stared into my eyes.

"Heleyne, what did you do?"

His face didn't reflect the fear that I had just seen on some of the other faces, but he was cautious, anxious. They had all just seen me heal a young dying boy with my bare hands. I had no good answer for him.

What the hell had I done?

CHAPTER THIRTEEN

"Yes, Heleyne, what did you do?" Guinevere's voice was severe and my mouth dropped open in surprise. She leaned over me, her eyebrows pulled together in consternation.

"I told you to stay behind me and keep your eye out for Arthur, not to bound ahead and interfere with the fighting. Helping that young boy was commendable, Heleyne, but you could have gotten us both killed."

I realized that she was trying to help by diverting Lucan's anger towards herself instead of me. But it had been clear to all who had witnessed it, including Lucan, that she was the one who could have gotten killed. Her statement only seemed ridiculous. Lucan stared at her in bemusement.

"Your highness, with all due respect, Heleyne was behind you. Although to be honest, my question for her was concerned not with her logistical placement, but with her healing abilities."

"I don't see why that matters," Guinevere sniffed. "Heleyne disregarded my order. We were only trying to find Arthur to give him this," she explained, dangling a golden cross on a chain in front of Lucan's face. I had no idea where she had conjured it from… but it was Arthur's lucky crucifix. Everyone knew that he seldom went anywhere without it.

"I needed to get this to Arthur," she continued. "In his current state, he forgot it. But you did a noble thing," she nodded at me. "Helping that boy up after getting stabbed likely saved him from getting trampled."

"Helping that boy up?" Lucan raised his eyebrows. "That boy was at death's door and then Heleyne knelt beside him and all of a sudden, he was fine. I wish to know how that was possible."

"I... um. I did nothing really," I answered meekly. "I simply held my hands against his wound, slowing the flow of blood. I think it gave him a spare moment to gain his bearings and then he felt fine enough to stand. That is all, my love."

I turned to Guinevere. "And I'm so sorry for my thoughtlessness, your highness." I forced the words from my stubborn lips. "I did not mean to cause you worry or distress. I simply wished to help the little boy."

Guinevere smoothed her face into a calm and loving expression. "Of course I forgive you, dear girl. I know you only meant the best for the young squire. Come now. Let us return to the castle and allow Sir Lucan to return to the battle. Think nothing more of it." She handed the crucifix to Lucan. "Sir Lucan, if you could safely deliver this pendant to the king, I would be most grateful."

I could see the wavering in Lucan's eyes as he purveyed the queen. He wanted to believe her, I could tell. Finally, he shook his head and took the necklace from Guinevere.

"Of course," he replied. "I'll hand it to him myself, your highness." She nodded.

Lucan set me gently down and stared into my eyes. "Can you walk?" he asked softly. I nodded.

"I'm fine, Luc. Really. I think the sight of the blood and fighting just overwhelmed me and I felt faint. I'm fine now."

"Your good deed should not go unnoticed," he observed, although he still sounded unsure. "I shall speak to Arthur about it."

"There is no need for that," I replied quickly. "I only did what anyone else would do."

Lucan smiled, his white teeth glinting in the moonlight. "So humble," he replied. "Very well. I'll walk you to your horses and send an escort back with you to the palace."

We quickly made our way to Guinevere's mount and Lucan lifted us both onto the horse, instructing four nearby soldiers to personally accompany us back to the palace. With a quick kiss, he dropped the visor to his helmet and rushed back off into the fray. I sighed. He had always been a warrior. He thrived in these situations.

Guinevere nudged Flower into a gallop and we made quick time back the winding road to the castle gates. Once there, my mother sent the soldiers back to assist the others and we entered the quiet, safe darkness of the palace fortress.

We slid to the ground and led Flower back to the stables, handing her reigns to a stern Reagan, before making our way back to our bedchambers. I accompanied Guinevere to hers first, helping her out of her gown and into a nightgown before I made my way back to my own chambers.

Too weary to face the long line of buttons on the back of my gown, I sighed and envisioned myself dressed in a cotton nightgown. Immediately, I was and my green velvet gown was hanging neatly in my armoire.

Crossing the room to the open windows, I leaned my forehead against the cool stone bricks as I gazed down the mountainside. I could see the torches that the soldiers carried flickering in the night even from here. Somehow, it gave me a sense of comfort, seeing them move and burn. Lucan was there with them and the fire marked where he traveled. Somehow, even though it was irrational, I felt as though if those torches were burning brightly, then Lucan was safe and well.

"What have you done?"

I startled at the calm voice and turned.

Lachesis, the middle sister of the Fates, was sitting on my bed, silently observing me. I glanced at the moon outside. It was nowhere near midnight.

I swallowed my annoyance at her habit of appearing in my bedchambers and crossed the room to stand in front of her, determined to act meek, as though I had no idea of the power that I actually wielded.

"I'm sorry, Lachesis," I murmured innocently. "I thought the time to meet you was midnight. Am I late?"

"No," she replied coolly. "But you have misbehaved. And I would like to know why."

"I don't know what you mean," I answered, leveling my gaze at her pale face.

In the moonlight, she appeared even paler than normal, her milky skin almost transparent. Her white-blonde hair flowed down her back, her lips plump and red. She could appear in any form that she wished, but this was her favorite. I found that I preferred it to the frightening hag that she truly was.

"Yes, you do," she contradicted. "You used your bloodstone to heal someone, a boy. Why?"

I tried to conceal my surprise. How in the world did she know that already?

"It was an accident," I answered quickly. "I have no idea what happened. One moment I was kneeling beside him, only to check on his wound, and the next moment, he was healed. I have no idea what happened."

I prayed that I was convincing, that she would think that I had inadvertently and innocently tapped into goddess power without realizing it...and that I thought it was simply the power of the bloodstone.

She studied my face, probing my thoughts, trying to ascertain my sincerity. Finally, her gaze broke and I knew that I had passed this test. She believed me. I had successfully outsmarted one of the Fates... something that was unheard of. I breathed a small sigh of relief.

"You should have been more careful," she admonished me. "You know that your bloodstone is powerful. You could have accidentally revealed yourself to your daedal."

I inwardly groaned. It was difficult to continue this charade, almost painful, but I did my best to look meek.

"You're right," I acknowledged carefully. "I'll certainly be more careful next time." Lachesis scowled in my direction.

"There will not be a next time," she snapped.

And with that, in a flash, she transformed into the stooped ancient hag that she was. Her back was hunched grotesquely, her hair white and stringy. Her face, however, was the worst. It looked like cracked gray porcelain. A thousand tiny web-like wrinkles began at her forehead and radiated to her chin, making her look like a corpse. I gasped, more out of surprise than actual fear and she smiled, stepping toward me, with eyes so faded that they looked like clouds.

"Do I frighten you, Heleyne?" she asked throatily, reaching out to run one twisted finger down my cheek, trailing onto my neck. I steeled myself and remained still, enduring her frigid touch. She was as cold as a corpse, just as Alexi and Cadmus were. Horror squeezed my heart. Was she soulless as well?

She felt my sudden apprehension and cocked her head, her wrinkled hand frozen on my shoulder. I felt a chill, but against all odds, managed to not move and kept my feet planted on the floor. She was the epitome of unnerving.

"You're such a proud one, little keeper," she murmured into my ear. Her frosty breath hissed against my skin as her voice chilled my heart. Everything about her screamed *danger*. It raised the hair on my neck and she smiled.

"There will not be a next time because you will not be here to make another mistake," she announced coldly. Alarm caused my heart to pound wildly against my ribcage. The Fates had never done this before.

"What do you mean?" I asked shakily. "I must be here. I know my Daedal better than anyone. No one can handle her like I can."

She nodded thoughtfully. "Yes, in the past that has been the case," she agreed. "But you have shown that you are losing your edge. Ahmose will handle her. You will come with me. The people here will simply fear that you have been taken by intruders and they will search for you for awhile, but in the end, it will be as though you never existed here at all."

My heart thudded so loudly that I could hear it in the still night and I knew she could too. I had to think quickly, to get her to change her mind, but I couldn't come up with a feasible retort. After a moment, I managed to think of something to stall.

"What will you do with me?"

With nimble quickness that I would never have thought that she possessed, she bounded back to my side, throwing me against the wall with supernatural strength. With my head shoved against the hard stone, she sniffed at my face, my neck, my arms, my legs. All the while, her white hair straggled down her back over her arms and I could feel the evil emanating from her.

How I had never felt it when I had been in mortal form? It was thick in the air around her. Even a mortal should recognize her for the threat that she was, yet I never did. I had always wanted to believe her. As she pushed her face into mine, I ached to throw her off, to use my goddess strength to defend myself, but I couldn't. I couldn't reveal myself in such a way and so instead, I gritted my teeth as she continued to sniff at me.

Shoving my nightgown up, she licked my inner thigh, dragging her rough, cold tongue along the skin of my knee to the juncture of my thighs. She paused there, with her face buried in my nether region, keeping me pressed to her with one cold arm. With her other hand, she used her long thumb nail to rip the bodice of my nightgown and push it away, leaving me exposed and naked as the light cotton material fell to the ground.

Goosebumps formed on every surface of my body in the night breeze, but I stood still, trying to force my face to remain expressionless as I willed my heart to calm. Glancing up at me, Lachesis lingered over my belly before moving to my heart, pressing her ear to my ribcage and listening, holding her icy hands against my shoulder blades, before she licked the skin between my breasts.

Burying her face between them, she inhaled, then turned her head to listen once again. I held my breath, willing my heart, which was so close to her ear, to slow down. I didn't want to tip my hand, because she would expect me to be frightened in this mortal body, but she didn't need to know how much she truly unnerved me, either.

"So proud," she murmured, leaving my breasts to pay close attention to my arm. Lifting it, first she examined it and then she sniffed at it, following an invisible trail from my shoulder to my wrist. When she finally reached my pulse point, she froze with her nose against my skin. I felt my blood pulsing hard as my heart beat against her mouth.

"You're lying about something, Keeper," she observed. "I can smell it. Along with your fear, I sense deceit. What are you hiding?"

Her cloudy eyes pierced mine as she stayed poised above my wrist. I fought to remain calm. This was the most unsettling situation I had ever been in. She was purposely violating my personal dignity and there wasn't a thing that I could do about it. Or that I *should* do about it, anyway.

"Nothing, Lachesis," I whispered. "I am lying about nothing. I am hiding nothing."

"You lie," she snarled and plunged her yellowed teeth into my wrist. I gasped and cried out, but rigidly kept my feet planted and forced myself to remain calm and frozen in place as the ancient witch drank my blood.

I couldn't take my eyes off of her face. Her eyes were closed in pleasure as my blood streaked from the corners of her mouth. I could see the pulse beating in my arm, the vital blood pumping faster into her mouth with every second that I became more frightened. With every second, I felt weaker as she took more and more of my blood into her mouth.

"Stop," I murmured calmly. "Lachesis, stop. What are you doing?"

I had never been more proud of myself for exhibiting restraint. My mind was whirling and I wanted nothing more than to throw this old woman across the room. Yet I stood limply and allowed her to suck my very life away. There wasn't anything else I could without tipping my hand.

Seconds turned into minutes and my body had begun to feel cold from blood loss before Lachesis finally complied with my request and dropped my arm, taking one step back.

I gripped my wrist with my other hand tightly as I stared at her.

My blood streaked down her chin and her eyes were no longer cloudy. They were shiny and black and had a slightly crazed look in them as she studied me.

"You are lying, Harmonia. I tasted it." *Harmonia.*

Once again, my heart stilled with fear. Her eyes were shiny and glazed with pleasure, but in them was knowledge. *She knew everything.* She had drunk my blood to taste for lies. And I couldn't control that. My own blood had given me away. She knew the truth.

I returned her stare coldly as she continued to study me.

"How can this be?" she asked. "What is the meaning of this?"

"Do you think that you are the only ones who control Fate?" I asked humorlessly. "You are not. We have simply allowed you to hold that role … and for far too long. That will end soon."

"Will it?" she replied with icy, eerie calm.

I took a step toward her, intent on restraining her, on holding her down until I could decide what to do, but she took a long step back.

With a strange and horrible screech, she thrust her head and shoulders back and her clothing fell to shreds and dropped to the ground around her ankles. As she stood naked, her wrinkled skin turned ebony black and hideous bony wings ripped from her body, fanning to fill that entire side of the room. She opened her eyes and they were blood red.

"Will it?" she asked again, her voice hoarse and dripping with the evil that I knew she was. The temperature in the room plummeted, the cold radiating from Lachesis herself. I shivered, as the hair raised at the nape of my neck. I could see every quick pant of breath that I took hanging in the air.

Glancing down, I saw that her toes had turned into razor sharp talons, scratching the floor as she took a few more steps. Then suddenly, she took flight through the room, shooting over my head and out my open windows.

Rushing to my balcony, I watched as she flew quickly from the palace and into the night. In horror, I realized that a long, scaly tail hung behind her. And then she was gone and I was alone, breathing hard as I leaned against the balcony railing.

What did this mean? Where was she going? *What the hell was she?*

I desperately tried to calm myself but dizziness from fear, from the blood loss, from the shock of what had just happened overtook me and I crumpled to the ground in a heap.

My tattered clothes lay in a pile in front of me and I concentrated on them as I sent out a silent plea for help.

Mother, I need you.

And then I closed my eyes.

CHAPTER FOURTEEN

"Help her! Help her, Hecate," a voice pleaded anxiously.

My mother. I tried to open my eyes but my eyelids were too heavy. It felt as though a brick lay on each one. I struggled with it for a moment and then gave up. I didn't have the strength to move or to speak. All I could do was listen.

"Hecate, what has happened?" Ares muttered hurriedly. He was anxious as well. I could hear it in his voice. "What is wrong with her?"

Where was I? Was I still in my bedchambers? I inhaled a breath and in it, I could taste the roses that drifted in on the breeze from the gardens. I was still in Camelot, that was certain. The night air was thick with roses and brambles. I could smell the damp earth from outside and the moss that covered the palace walls and I could feel the salt from the sea on my lips.

What was wrong with me? I was physically drained, my energy gone. I couldn't lift my hands or move my legs. I could hear Hecate rustling beside me, moving, perhaps mixing something. Glass and metal scraped against each other and then a pungent odor filled the room, clinging to the inside of my nostrils.

"What the hell is that?" Ares boomed.

"Hush, Ares," my mother cautioned.

"I care not who hears me," Ares thundered. "I wish to know what the witch is going to feed my daughter. It smells like death."

"Perhaps that is exactly what it is, war god," Hecate muttered. "You do not need to know what my magic contains, only that it is very powerful. Lachesis drank from your daughter's blood. You can see the wound in her arm for yourself. Your daughter's pure blood has now fueled the Moirae. But because of that, it has left Harmonia impotent and spent.

"I shall have to use strong magic to revive her. Do not worry yourself, Ares. I've used this very potion on others, including your other daughter, Ortrera. She came through just fine and so will Harmonia...and her baby."

Something cool forced my lips open and the most vile liquid I had ever tasted dripped down my throat, sliding into my belly like fire. The repugnant potion churned within my stomach, rapidly spreading through my blood with every beat of my heart. I felt it return my strength and as it did, it forced a shrill scream from my lungs, jerking my body into a sitting position as I shrieked.

Guinevere clapped her hands over her ears as she stared at me in panic.

"Harmonia, stop!" she murmured. "Are you alright?"

I quieted the unconscious scream and assessed myself. Was I?

"I don't know," I answered. "I think so."

Hecate patted my arm. "You'll be fine now. Our concerns should not be with your well being, but with Lachesis... and what she has done with her new knowledge."

"What do you mean?" I asked anxiously.

Hecate stared at me patiently. The sympathy that I found in her gaze was startling and I inhaled.

"What is it?" I asked quickly. "What has happened?"

She sighed and my parents drew closer, making me instantly nervous. I wasn't sure if they meant to restrain me or comfort me.

"As you know," she began, "Whenever someone travels time, there is a risk... a risk that something will be altered. Any change, no matter how small, can cause massive ripple effects, effects that start small, but gradually widen until they create devastatingly large changes."

I kept my eyes trained on Hecate's solemn face.

"What has happened?" I repeated in a whisper.

"Close your eyes and hold hands," she instructed quietly. We quickly did as she asked and our minds were instantly filled with visions.

The world had turned black.

Everything was just like the Wastelands where Cadmus was being held... void and cold. I shivered as I watched the images unfold in my mind.

Mortals were heartless, war raged everywhere. Thunderous dark clouds encapsulated every city as far as my mind could see. It was a bleak place and it was because of the Fates. I knew that without doubt. Because they did not have to continue their charade in order to keep me contained, they had turned the world into what they wanted it to be. Their only purpose now was to find the sword. They did not care what happened to the mortals. And the mortals were killing themselves.

Even the Spiritlands were dark and Olympus was ravaged and war torn. Houses were demolished, the land was quiet and black, the people were miserable.

I gasped and yanked my hands away, ending the visions. I jumped from my bed and rushed to the windows. The lush rolling mountainside below me had turned brown and dead. Black clouds swirled overhead, while dry leaves and withered rose petals blew across the countryside.

"What will happen?" I cried. "What can we do?"

Hecate studied me sadly. "I know not," she admitted softly. "This is like nothing that I've ever seen. They have changed everything. But we must repair it. If we do not, I fear that everything will be lost."

"That is not an answer, witch," I glared at her. "I only need to know what to do. Point me in the right direction and I will gladly do what I need to do." As I glanced around at my mother, father and Hecate, I realized something. Lucan was not here.

"Where's Lucan?" I asked hesitantly. "Ares, you are back from the skirmish. Where is Lucan?"

Ares shifted his weight and glanced at my mother. She looked pained as she studied me.

"Harmonia...." her voice trailed off.

"What?" I asked in alarm. "Just tell me. What has happened?"

Guinevere pushed her shoulders back and cleared her throat. "He's in the dungeons."

"The dungeons?" I cried. "Why? What the hell is going on?"

Ares stepped forward. "Your parlor trick," he explained quietly. "You saved the young squire in front of an entire group of soldiers and then Lucan carried you away. They're crying witchcraft and claiming that Lucan was involved."

"Lucan... but that's insane," I stuttered. "But what about me? I'm the one who did it- why am I still here and Lucan is confined to the dungeon?"

"Well, that's a little tricky," Ares shook his head. "Hecate froze time."

I stared at him blankly. "Hecate did what?"

Hecate interjected. "I froze time. We needed to meet to decide what to do. Everything can still be salvaged, but we will need Zeus' sword to do it. We cannot rectify anything at all if they burn you for a witch, Harmonia."

The mental image of being tied to a stake and burned alive caused me to shudder. How did I get myself into such messes?

"I see," I replied. "So then, witch, what do you propose that we do? My mother believes that the sword might be hidden at the king's parents' property somewhere, but we know not exactly where. How do we find it? And what about me? They want me dead. Surely, though, Arthur will listen to reason. He knows me. He knows that I am not a witch."

Again, they stared at each other uncertainly.

"Harmonia, everything has drastically changed. Not only has the world itself changed, but the people here have changed as well, products of that environment. Arthur is… not the same," Ares explained.

I raised an eyebrow, trying desperately to conceal my alarm. "Meaning?"

"Meaning that Arthur is not currently the warm, good-hearted person that you know him to be. He has grown cold much like everyone else here. He's as ruthless as anyone I've ever seen," Ares admitted.

"No," I shook my head. "I don't believe that from him. He's the most compassionate man I've ever known."

"He was," my mother agreed. "But no longer. Not right now. The boy who you saved? Arthur ran him through with his lance… he didn't want a person tainted by witchcraft to live."

I gasped. The image of the sweet boy's face passed through my mind and I flinched at the thought of Arthur killing him. This couldn't be happening. I shook my head.

"It's true, daughter," Ares confirmed. "I was there and I saw it myself."

"So what do we do?" I asked limply.

"We get the sword," my mother replied simply. "It's the only thing we can do."

"I suggest that we free Lucan from the dungeons," Ares offered. "Harmonia, you and he should ride to find the sword. We don't want to leave him here- we don't want them to execute him before you return with the sword."

I nodded, finally able to suppress my panic. If we had a plan, I was fine. I could work with a plan. And there was no way in hell that I would leave Lucan here alone.

"Ares and I will remain here," my mother continued. "We'll try to contain this situation as best we can. But this goes without saying... you need to find the sword quickly. It is hard to say what the Fates will do in the meantime, daughter."

I nodded solemnly. She had never been more correct.

"I will accompany you," Hecate added quietly. "We no longer need to be quite so careful about making changes here- we will change everything back to its rightful place with the sword. You will need my assistance."

Ares agreed. "That is a wise idea, witch. You will protect my daughter with your life." It wasn't a suggestion or a request. It was a bold imperative. I shot Hecate an *I'm sorry* look behind my father's back. She shrugged understandingly.

"I will do what I can," she replied. Ares glared at her, indicating that her best was not enough. She ignored it, turning instead to face me.

WITH MY LAST BREATH

"So, first we need to free Lucan," I pointed out. "And then we will ride out."

"It won't be difficult," Ares said. "Time has stopped here. We will walk into the dungeons, I'll break his chains and we'll … in fact, let us not talk about it. Let us just do it." He waved his meaty hand and we were all standing in the front of the dungeon's iron gates.

The smell from the dungeons was moldy and stale and my nose automatically wrinkled. It was eerily quiet. Nothing moved, even the air was still. It was as though we were walking through a paused movie. It was the strangest feeling.

Ares shoved his fist through the metal keyhole of the gate and it tumbled impotently to the floor, clanging loudly against the stone. He pushed the gates open and motioned for us to continue through.

"Ladies first," he grinned.

I rolled my eyes and walked past, anxious to find Lucan. He should not be in this place. This was a place for murderers and thieves.

The darkness down here was blinding- it took a few minutes for my eyes to adjust. Torches were few and far between. I could hear Hecate muttering beneath her breath, but I couldn't understand what she was saying and frankly, at this point, I just didn't care. My sole focus was on Lucan.

Turning into a long, damp hallway, we began looking into cells. Dank and dark, these were miserable little holes used for housing the scourge of Camelot's society. I cringed away from the walls. Inside each cell, a dirty, hardened criminal was frozen.

Some were chained in corners, some were hanging in chains from the ceiling and one, a particularly dangerous looking man, was standing frozen with his fingers wrapped around his cell bars. His legs were manacled and bleeding onto the floor. His icy blue eyes stared sightlessly at me and I unconsciously moved away.

"He's here!" Ares called from the front. I hurried to catch up.

Breaking through the cell doors, Ares rushed inside. I gasped as I turned the corner to follow him. My beloved was dangling in mid-air, his wrists bleeding as the manacles cut into his skin. His face was bruised and blood dripped down his bare toes onto the stone bricks.

Tears welled up as I rushed to him, my eyes stinging. Ares was already lowering him from the ceiling onto the floor.

"Wake him," he implored to Hecate. "Wake him and leave here. Don't awaken anyone else until you have passed the palace gates."

She nodded. "That's the plan, war god. I can only keep time still for so long, but a few more minutes shouldn't be a problem."

I knelt next to my husband, stroking his battered face.

"Why did they do this?" I whispered. "Why did they beat him? He's a valued knight. Arthur loves him."

"Arthur *loved* him," Guinevere corrected. "He doesn't love anything anymore. Everything has changed, daughter."

Cold fingers curled around my belly. "I can't leave you here, then," I murmured to her while I stroked Lucan's bloody hand. "What will he do to you?"

"Nothing," she replied, meeting my gaze calmly. "He will do nothing to me. You were the one who healed the boy. He has no reason to suspect that I am anything other than his wife."

"But you said that he doesn't love anything now. What about you? He loved you more than life."

She shook her head sadly. "He's empty, dear one. He loves nothing. He has been hardened to the world. But he won't harm me- I've given him no reason. Just find the sword and return so that we can fix this atrocity. No one here deserves this."

I nodded, listening to Hecate mumbling her incantations as she hovered over my husband.

"There is one detail," Hecate muttered, looking up at me, "That I haven't told you."

"And that is?"

"He cannot remember you. If I bring him back just as he is, he would never leave here. He would stay to try and clear his name. I will take his memories and return them to him later."

Dejection filled the pit of my stomach, heavy and cold. I was sick of being in positions where my husband didn't remember me. He was mine and he should know that he was mine. But I understood the need for it now and nodded silently. Hecate returned her attention to Lucan.

"Awake," she whispered finally. "Awake, awake, awake."

His eyes opened, his beautiful warm, dark eyes. He focused on me since I was directly in front of him. There was not an ounce of recognition in his gaze and I steeled myself, feeling overwhelmed by déjà vu. I had been in this situation once before in Eris' house in the Spiritlands.

He stared at all of us in turn, remaining still and silent on the cold, stone floor as he studied his surroundings. Finally, he spoke.

"What are we doing here?"

Hecate answered him calmly with a question. "Do you know who you are?"

He shook his head. "And I do not know you, either. Should I?"

She smiled gently, patting his hand. "Not right now, but you will later. For now, we need to move. Can you walk?"

He gingerly stretched his injured limbs, flinching just a little from the pain before he quickly masked it. His warrior's heart had not changed. He was not going to allow us to see how much he hurt. I wanted to smile, but didn't. Nothing about this situation was funny. My soul mate had been beaten within an inch of his life and he didn't remember me. It wasn't funny at all.

I rushed forward to offer my assistance while he stood, but he shrugged me off. I should have expected that- he would never lean on a woman, even when he didn't remember who he was. He picked himself off of the floor and stood quietly, assessing each of us with clear eyes.

"Let us go," Hecate suggested. "We need to hurry."

Lucan didn't ask any questions, he simply accompanied us up and out of the dungeon and through the palace until we stood outside in the darkened courtyard. As we passed a commons area, we found soldiers frozen in mid-movement-armor dangling in midair, horses halted mid-step. Lucan turned to us in amazement and confusion.

"What is going on here? What is this?" he asked, gesturing with his arm. "What trickery is this?"

"It's no trickery," I replied quietly. "But there is no time to explain. We'll explain it from the safety of the road."

He studied me for a moment before offering me a curt nod.

"Very well."

We hurried into the stables and saddled three horses. Aphrodite and Ares lingered inside the stable doors, watching us prepare. Reagan was frozen mid-stroke as he wiped down a damp horse. Beads of sweat ran down its great head and dripped onto the floor, several drops frozen in the air.

As we mounted, Ares spoke.

"Hurry, daughter. Return as soon as you can."

I gave him a droll look. "Obviously."

As we passed my parents, my mother grabbed Celine's bridle and leaned up toward me. "Be careful, sweetling," she murmured. "Hurry back."

I nodded, bending to brush a kiss across her cheek.

Hecate looked back at me.

"Are you ready? We must hurry. I cannot hold it back any longer."

"Yes. Let us ride."

We nudged our horses into a run and we galloped through the commons and out the palace doors. I felt Celine's strength welling in her thick muscles beneath me as she surged forward, her ears flicking from time to time. Even the horses sensed that something was amiss.

When we were halfway down the mountain, I heard the castle above us erupt into noise. The spell had been broken-time was unfrozen and everyone was awake. It was a jarring comparison, showing just how quiet it really had been while everyone was silent.

Lucan glanced sideways at me, giving me a long look as we rode hard to escape the palace.

"Can you explain now, my lady?" he called.

"Yes," I called back. "Just as soon as I think of something to say."

He threw his head back and laughed, a sound that warmed my soul. No matter what we had to go through or how many times he didn't remember me, he was the same and so was I. That was all that mattered.

CHAPTER FIFTEEN

We sat around a flickering campfire, the orange and red flames licking upwards toward the night and I stared at Lucan's face through them. Without his knowledge, Hecate had bewitched our horses' legs, enabling them to carry us farther than humanly possible away from the castle grounds. He didn't even notice, engrossed in my feeble attempts to explain our predicament away.

In the darkness, Hecate nudged me.

"Here," she pushed something toward me. "Drink this. We'll need you at full strength."

I glanced down at a gleaming nickel flask. She had brought nectar from the Spiritlands. Drinking it would maintain my immortal strength... and oh, how I wished I could share it with Lucan. But glancing at him, I knew that I could not. His face was pensive as he reflected across the campfire. He wasn't ready to hear the truth.

"When should we tell him?" I whispered, confident that the crackles and pops of the fire would hide my question from him.

"Not yet," she replied thoughtfully. "Not yet."

I nodded as I lifted the flask to my lips, taking a sip of the sumptuous liquid. Spiritlands nectar was the most delicious substance in the world, even if it was created from the blood of the unborn. I closed my eyes and enjoyed the overwhelming sensations as my strength returned to my limbs. I felt it flowing in my blood, warm and fierce.

"So where are we going?" Lucan asked. I opened my eyes to find him watching me, his dark eyes sharp and perceptive. I should have known. He never missed anything.

I rose from the blanket that I was seated on and crossed to his side, perching in the sand next to him. The wind gently blew, wafting his scent in my direction, and it was all I could do not to launch myself into his arms.

"We must travel to Brittany," I explained. "There is something there that we feel the King needs."

"And how would you know what the king needs?" Lucan asked me with a raised eyebrow.

"I just do," I murmured. "Can you trust me?"

He stared down at me, the bronzed angles of his face catching the firelight. His eyes were so deep that I felt I could fall into them.

"Possibly," he answered. "I feel as though I should, but I have nothing to base that feeling on."

"Knights must often trust their instincts, correct?" He had told me as much many times.

"But alas, you have told me that I am no longer a knight," he answered dejectedly. "And I cannot remember why."

"It is through no fault of your own," I assured him. "And we will work hard to put things to rights. Your assistance will be of utmost help."

He nodded. "And you will have it. I shall do what I can."

My heart ached at the pain on his face. Lucan was loyalty and honor at its finest. It must be crushing him now to believe that the king had dismissed him from duty. I longed to reach out and stroke the pain away, to hold him close, but I swallowed hard instead, gripping my own hands in my lap. *I must not.*

"I think I will turn in," I said as I rose. "We will have a long ride in the morning."

Hecate and Lucan also rose and made preparations to sleep. We encircled our campground in a ring of fire in order to keep wolves away while we slept and laid our thick saddle blankets on the ground to sleep on.

"I'll take first watch," Lucan offered. "I am not tired yet, anyway."

From the weary lines on his face, I knew he was lying. But it would do no good to argue. He would never let a woman take first watch.

"Very well," I answered. "Thank you. I'll take it second."

I snuggled down into my saddle blanket and tried to sleep, ignoring the horse smell that emanated from it. Pulling my cloak around me, I discreetly watched Lucan. He stared into the night with alert eyes, studying any small noise with the utmost care. He held a sword on his lap. No matter where we were, he made me feel safe.

I meant to stay awake as well, but the warmth of the fire lulled me to sleep. My eyelids became so heavy that I simply couldn't hold them open. But no sooner had I closed them, then I was standing in the Wastelands.

The harsh wind shrieked around me and the whiteness was startling… swirling with shades of black and gray. It was the strangest place I'd ever been. The cold penetrated me from the outside in and I stood shivering as I watched for Cadmus.

"Where are you?" I called into the vast empty space. "You've called me here… where are you?"

There was no answer but for the howl of the wind. I pulled my cloak more tightly around my face.

"Cadmus!" I called. "Please answer me! I don't like it here."

"No one does," a voice replied. I turned and found Ahmose standing behind me. His black eyes glittered as he perused me.

"Cadmus is no longer here," he told me, staring at me as though I should have already known.

"Where is he?" I asked, my heart leaping into my throat. "Where did he go? And if he's not here, who brought me here? You?"

Ahmose nodded. "Yes, I brought you here, Harmonia. Everything has been changed. Have I taught you nothing over the years?"

"I don't understand," I whimpered. "What do you mean?"

"You changed everything," Ahmose repeated sternly. "Everything that has happened is because of your carelessness. How could you let Lachesis know that you were in Camelot, that you knew everything? How could you be so careless?"

"Wait… did you know?" Something in his voice told me that he did.

"Of course I did. I've been with you for a very long time. I knew, but I was willing to be patient and wait until you trusted me enough to tell me. But you didn't and now everything is in ruins."

"Don't say that!" I shouted. "I'm going to fix it. Everything."

He shook his head sadly. "I don't know that you can. Even a tiny ripple in time has massive consequences. I've told you that before. But this… this is no ripple. This is a jagged tear. Everything has been changed. There is no comprehending the consequences from this."

"Can I trust you?" I asked him. "They kill you, you know. Eventually, they will torture you to your death."

"Yes," he murmured. "I know. I always knew it. They will torture me because I will protect you. I saw that long ago," he shrugged. "But that will not happen now. Not unless you manage to change our current course. Are you willing to do that?"

"Of course I'm willing!" I snapped. "I will do whatever it takes. Can you tell me what to do?"

"No," he replied. "But I can give you something. Something that I already gave you and you allowed it to slip back into their grasp."

"The box!" I gasped.

He nodded. "Yes. The box of murderous souls. This will be the second time that I sacrifice myself for you, Keeper. When they realize that it is gone and that I am missing, they will realize what I have done. And they will hunt me down until they find me. Fix this before that happens," he implored me. "Save us all."

"Cadmus is in this box," he told me. "His soul will be in your hands. If something happens to it while he is separated from his body, it will permanently be so. Take great care."

My heart pounded loudly. Cadmus was in the box.

"What do I do?" I cried. "What am I supposed to do with the box?"

He thrust it into my hands. "Save us all," he answered simply.

"I want to. I'll try, but…"

But he was gone. I was standing in the Wastelands alone and there was no one left to answer my questions. I clutched the intricate carved black box and closed my eyes, willing myself to wake.

And then I was. I opened my eyes to the blackness of night in Camelot. The box of souls was in my hands. I stroked the textured top. My husband's soul was trapped in my hands and there was currently nothing I could do about it. I'd never felt so helpless in my life. I lay still for a few minutes, trying to collect myself.

"Are you awake?" Lucan asked softly from his vantage point across the fire.

I sat up and nodded. "Yes. I... grew cold. I couldn't sleep." I opened my knapsack and placed the box gently inside.

"I'm not tired," he told me. "Feel free to try to go back to sleep. You should rest. As you said, tomorrow will be long and tiresome."

I studied him, my heart heavy in my chest. He was so beautiful and strong. And if I couldn't think of what to do or how to save us, then everything that he was would end here in this life. Once he died here, since his soul was trapped in a box, he would be no more. And what a horrible, horrible tragedy that would be for the world. He was a beautiful person.

"I don't think I can," I replied. "I'm so cold. Do you... do you mind if I come and sit by you so that I can share your warmth?"

He looked at me for a moment, studying my face. What I had requested was very brazen for these times, something a lady would never do. But I wasn't a lady. I was a goddess and I would do whatever the hell I felt like doing.

"Of course," he finally replied. "You may share my warmth."

Picking up my knapsack, I crept to his side and settled in, curling up next to him with my bag clutched in my arms. Being here, next to this man who normally knew me better than I even knew myself, was comforting. It was like being home. And to a girl who had traveled through a thousand different lives and bodies over the years, it was heaven. I closed my eyes and slept.

CHAPTER SIXTEEN

The sound of a dry twig breaking woke me and my eyes popped open. I was alone, both Lucan and Hecate were nowhere to be found. I sat straight up, the box of souls still in my arms, as looked around.

It was early morning and the fire had died down to embers. Everything but my blanket had been packed up and was waiting to be loaded onto our horses. I shook my head slightly to clear the sleep from it.

Another twig popped and I spun around, finding Lucan walking toward me.

"You should be glad I pose no threat," he observed. "You sleep like the dead."

He was right. I really did. But I knew, I had always known, that he would protect me from any bumps in the night. Not that I could say that to him right now. Instead, I gazed around.

"Where is Hecate?" I asked.

"I'm here!" she called, approaching us from the left. "I was hunting for some breakfast."

My mouth twitched. "Really?" I smiled. "And what, domestic goddess, did you find?"

"Don't doubt me," she shot back. "Do plump, ripe blackberries appeal to you?"

"They do sound delicious," I admitted. "Do you know anyone who could find some for us?"

She glared at me, swinging a basket full of berries that I knew she had probably conjured. This witch had not walked over the countryside to find berries. I knew that much to be true.

She handed them to Lucan and he sat on the ground, offering them to me. I took a handful and put one in my mouth, enjoying the juicy rich taste. They weren't lotus blossoms, but they were delicious nonetheless. I licked the stickiness from my fingers before returning my attention to the witch.

"We should ride," Hecate muttered, looking in concern at the horizon. "They will approach us soon enough. We do not want to be here when they arrive. And I had a dream last night. There is a place I would like to stop along the way. I feel drawn to it even now."

Lucan stared at her curiously, but didn't ask any questions. He simply nodded.

"You're correct. We should ride far from here."

He reached down and offered me a hand, helping me to my feet. I stood face to face with him, his lips mere inches from my own, before he took a step backward.

"I readied your horse," he mumbled, gesturing toward Celine. "Everything is set."

I nodded and approached my horse, stroking her velvety nose for a moment before swinging up into the saddle. She was anxious and exhaled in short puffs, stomping her front foot.

"It's alright, Celine," I soothed her, patting her neck.

"No, it's not," Hecate contradicted. "It's really not. There is danger out there. I can sense it, the horses can sense it. We should be on our guard."

"And that we are," Lucan stated as he mounted his horse.

Following him, I nudged Celine into movement and we took off like streaks across the Camelot countryside. Behind us, heavy black clouds rolled and thunder rumbled throughout the land, but rain never came. The air, which was normally so damp and life-sustaining here, was now arid and empty.

Minutes turned into hours and I wished that we could simply envision that we were already there. But since Lucan still did not know who we really were, we could do no such thing. Instead, we rode our horses the traditional way and my backside was painfully aware of it. Piercing aches shot through my hips and with every jolt of the saddle, my lower back screamed.

As we traveled, I grew increasingly more appalled at the state of Camelot. Everything was dead. There was nothing vibrant or alive for as far as I could see. The once waving grasses were brown and wilted, rocks jutted from the craggy earth and dead trees hunched over on the horizon. It was as though the life had been sucked from the earth.

Finally, just when I thought that my back could take no more jolting from the saddle, something emerged from the dead landscape and Hecate shot forward. I kicked Celine into a gallop, anxious to stand on my feet again and to see where Hecate had brought us.

I slid from my horse and stretched happily for a moment, working out the kinks in my spine. Lucan came up from behind and caught the reins dangling from my hand.

"I'll take your horse, my lady," he offered. "You appear to be tired."

I nodded my thanks. "It has been a long time since I was in a saddle so long," I told him ruefully. "My back doesn't agree with this trip, apparently."

He smiled and together, we walked over the ridge. As we reached the top of the small hill, I stopped in my tracks. I knew this place from history books, for certain, but I also felt a strong vague recognition. I must have been here before.

Magnificent stone slabs rose from the ground in two rings. The outer ring was tall, and every two Sarsen stones were connected by a cap stone on top, linking them together. The inner ring was made from shorter bluestones. The stones were heavy and unlike their crumbling appearance in history books, they were pristine and straight.

We were at Stonehenge.

As we gazed upon it, a reverent hush overtook us. The place was magical, that much was certain. My bloodstone was practically buzzing against my breastbone and I felt the strongest urge to enter the rings. Strangely enough, even though everything else in the land was dead and brown, the grasses inside the ring were vibrant and alive, their green lushness reminding me of what Camelot was meant to be.

In the center, a wide, flat onyx stone was situated in the sun, glistening as the tiny flecks caught the light. It had been buffed and polished until it was perfectly smooth and I realized with a start that it was an altar. It had never been pictured in history books, because it simply wasn't there anymore. But it was here now, rising proudly from the ground and my feet felt the urge to begin walking toward it.

"Do you feel that, Heleyne?" Hecate called as she moved to meet it. "Do you feel it?"

"Yes," I answered her and my voice carried across the open meadow, clear and loud. There was something here, something otherworldly that was rippling over me, skimming over my skin, causing my fingertips to tingle. I wasn't sure what it was, but it was powerful. That much was apparent.

As Hecate trailed her fingers along the black shiny stone, she muttered to herself.

"This place is important," she whispered. "But why?"

She stopped and laid her hands flat on the stone, closing her eyes as she tilted her face to the sun. Her blonde hair flew in the wind as she concentrated and I noticed with a start, that the wind actually picked up as she touched the stone. My skirts were whirling around my legs.

Lucan and I silently watched as Hecate moved her lips without making a sound. Her shoulders threw back, chest thrust out and her feet were rigid as she saw whatever visions that were being presented to her. The wind picked up into a howl, blowing the tall green grass at our feet into a churning circle. I subconsciously scooted closer to Lucan. It felt as though we were building toward something.

And then it stopped. The entire meadow grew eerily silent and Hecate opened her eyes. They were pitch black. I gasped as she turned slowly to face me. She opened her mouth to speak and her voice was not her own.

"Harmonia, daughter of Ares and Aphrodite?"

It was a man's voice, gravelly and hoarse. Someone was speaking through the witch. My heart picked up a few paces and Lucan reached over to grasp my hand. His eyes were wide, his face a picture of utter shock.

I nodded. "Yes. I am Harmonia."

"You are the Chosen One?"

"Yes," I answered quietly, glancing at my birthmark. At this moment, it felt more like a curse as I waited to see what horror I would be facing now.

"We've been waiting for you," Hecate creaked. "Approach."

She held out her hand, allowing it to linger midair, in a gesture of welcome. I took a tentative step, but Lucan pulled me back.

"My lady, I do not think you should," he worried. "We do not know what this is. I've never seen such a thing."

"Nor have I," I admitted. "But I must do it. There is much you don't understand, good knight. But you will in time."

I slipped my hand from his grasp, ignoring his anxious gaze and approached the altar. Hecate took my hand and assisted me onto it, pushing my shoulders until I lay down. Gazing upward, I stared at the gray sky and muted sun for a moment and then closed my eyes, waiting for something to happen.

Nothing.

I opened my eyes.

I was surrounded by ghosts. Hundreds of them were standing in ever-widening circles around us, dressed in clothing from many different ancient eras. Regardless of their differences, however, there was one thing they had in common. They were all warriors. Some were dressed in kilts, some were dressed in trousers, some wore armor, but they all held weapons.

The sky above us had turned black, blocking even the muted light from the sun. I knew I should be afraid, but I simply wasn't. I was only expectant, waiting to find out why they were here and what part I played in this. They had been waiting for me for a long time.

I looked to Hecate and found her eyes closed, but as I watched, a ghost stepped from her body. The voice. It detached itself from her and moved to my side.

He wore a fierce expression and I could see that his hair was dark red and he wore a shaggy beard. His eyes were black as night and he had a jagged scar running from the corner of his eye down to his pale chin. He reached a ghostly hand out and laid the heel of his palm on my forehead. The cold weight of it pushed my head to the stone beneath me.

"Close your eyes, young one," he commanded gruffly and I did as he requested, although I wasn't sure why.

Immediately, visions filled my head, and suddenly my mind was filled with many truths. Stonehenge had always been. Although no one knew who actually built it, it had always been whispered that Uther Pendragon, Arthur's father, had created it.

He had not. I saw that now. But he had used it as a burial ground for 460 great chiefs and warriors from Camelot after they had been slaughtered by Saxons in 410 AD. These were the men who surrounded me now, among many others.

I watched that battle quickly play out in my mind, watched the blood, the tears, the angst. I watched Uther burn their bodies here on the very altar that I was lying upon. And then my visions abruptly shifted. Different images flitted in and out, of many others who had been slain right where I was lying.

Pagans and druids were sacrificed here. The ancient priestesses felt the magic which emanated from this soil and they had used it as a place of sacrifice. I saw them standing on it, crying to the moon as they burned women alive.

Kings before Uther had used it as a sacred burial ground... I watched them offer eulogies before they burned the corpses here in the center of the ring. I could smell the smoke, the acrid scent of burning flesh as I watched.

And then the vision changed once more and I saw my mother. Strapped by leather cords, she was writhing in agony upon the stone. Blood ran from multiple wounds, dripping onto the stone and streaking onto the ground beneath her. I couldn't see the face of her assailant, and I craned my neck, trying to catch a glimpse. But it was too late. A sword plunged into her chest and she went still as her blood gushed freely around the blade.

I screamed, my eyes opening, but I was held to the altar by the ghost's cold hand.

"Stay still, Chosen One," he instructed. "You just saw what will happen if you do not act today. But there is still one more for you to see." Reluctantly, I closed my eyes once again.

This time, it was me on the stone. My face was pale, my cheeks were flushed. And then I realized something startling. I was wearing the same green velvet dress that I was currently wearing. Today, right now. My breathing stilled.

As I watched in horror, a small hand gripped the hilt of a sword and plunged it into my chest. I curled around it, my eyes opening wide, before I slumped once more back to the stone, my eyelids fluttering closed. As I watched, the child leaped to the altar beside me and covered me in an embrace, blood covering her small body. As she wept, her long hair dangled in the blood and it dripped from the ends of the strands. And then she turned her head and looked into my eyes.

Raquel.

My eyes popped open and I gasped.

"What was that?" I breathed. "Why?"

"There are many things that you do not know," the man replied. "Many things that were prophesied long ago and whispered down, generation from generation, but never written."

"But why?" I asked, staring into his black eyes.

"Because that is the way it has been," he said cryptically before he shrugged. "But you are here now. And now it will begin."

"What will begin?" I asked hesitantly. I watched Hecate and Lucan step forward so that they could hear his answer.

"Everything," he answered simply. "We would like our souls back. You have them. This once was my kingdom and it has fallen into evil, evil that it was not meant for. That troubles me. That troubles many of us here. We gave our lives, not for evil but for the good of our kingdom. Restore our souls and we will help you prevail."

"How?" I narrowed my eyes. "How can you help me?"

"Unlock our souls," he replied. "Set us free from our bondage in the underworld and we will ride together as an army to set this right. We will bring with us monsters from hell, beasts that we command. We can conquer the Fates here and set everything right."

He could sense my uncertainty. He moved closer, bending to add one more thing.

"Your husband," he began. "Can be saved if you trust me." His black eyes stared into mine, fierce and glistening and I swallowed hard.

I would do anything to save Cadmus. Anything. And that included trusting an army of undead warriors. But as I wavered, I also grew suspicious. If I unleashed beasts from hell, I had a feeling that they wouldn't want to return when the battle here was over. Who in their right mind would?

"And then what will you do?" I narrowed my eyes. "When this is over, what will you do?"

"Then we will rest," he answered simply. "Finally."

"Have your souls been at unrest this entire time?" I asked incredulously. He nodded.

"The Fates enjoy tampering with us," he replied angrily. "It pleases them. Please... allow us our revenge. It is said that you are the one."

Around me, the ghostly men began whispering, growing louder until their voices blended into a loud murmur, buzzing around me and echoing against the stones. I couldn't understand their words, but their chant was mesmerizing. I nodded.

"Yes," I finally said. "I will help you. And you will help me."

"Yes," he agreed.

He reached a cold hand down and grasped mine, helping me to stand. I motioned for Hecate and she quickly brought me my knapsack. I withdrew the black box of murderous souls from within it, holding it in my hands.

I studied it. There was a latch, but it was sealed closed. I had never considered that before, because knowing what it contained, I had never desired to open it. But now that I had a need, I could not see a way. I grew frustrated as I turned it over in my hands, searching every inch.

"You are the key," the ghostly chieftain told me quietly. "Your blood is the key."

My blood turned to ice in my veins as I stared at him.

"My blood? You mean, I must drip my blood onto it in order to open it?" I was confused.

But as I watched him, I felt icy fingers clench my stomach and I knew that wasn't the answer even before he shook his large head.

"No," he answered solemnly. "Your blood must spill. In order to open it, you must die."

CHAPTER SEVENTEEN

Hecate and Lucan gasped in unison as I clutched my hands to my stomach, unconsciously shielding my unborn baby.

"Die?" I breathed. "I must die?"

The chieftain nodded calmly. "You know that you cannot truly die but by Zeus' sword. But your mortal body here must die in order to unlock the trapped souls. You yourself will become displaced, just as we are now."

"Just as Cadmus is now," he added. "And you must trust us to bring you to victory, because your victory here will give you back your life. Your immortal life."

"That is quite a lot of trust," I observed, trying to still my racing heart. "And I do not know if I possess that much. I have an unborn child to think of now. And I know that if I die here, my soul will be in flux and I will forever be in eternal sleep, until the time when someone saves me."

"You will save yourself," he told me quietly. "Your unborn child is a part of you. When you are saved, so shall it be. Trust your instincts, Harmonia. You are the one."

"I wish that everyone would stop saying that," I replied angrily. "I am nothing but the child of gods. I am…"

"You are meant to take charge of your own destiny," he interrupted firmly. "So do it. Stand up and grab it with both of your hands. This is the only way."

"Don't!" Lucan cried from the edge of the circle, attempting to push through to get to me. "Heleyne, do not do it. There is no way to ensure that we will win. And if we do not, you will never be saved. Your soul will be lost."

But as I looked at him, at the way he was protective of me even now when he didn't know who I was to him, I knew that as long as he was dead to me, I was dead already. It sealed my decision.

"Yes," I murmured numbly. "I will do it."

I looked around the circle. "Who will do it?" I asked. "Who will kill me?"

Lucan was already shaking his head adamantly, intent on preventing it. Hecate stood beside him, her mouth pressed firmly shut, turning white at the corners. Her eyes were startled and she shook her head.

"Hecate, what is it?"

She shook her head slowly again, backing away from me. "I'm sorry, Harmonia. I didn't see it... I didn't know..."

But she knew now. Something that was troubling her so much that her eyes were full of pain and her hands were shaking. My body turned cold from fear and I took a step toward her.

"What?" I cried anxiously. "What is it that you didn't know?"

"It has to be her," she whispered. "She must be the one to do it or it will not work. She..."

I was panicked as I tried to make sense of what she was saying. Fear turned me immobile, however, and it felt as though I couldn't move.

"Who is *she*?" I asked hesitantly. "My mother?" It would kill my mother if she had to be the one. I wasn't sure that she could do it, which would mean that everyone would perish.

But Hecate shook her head quickly once more, her face a picture of dread.

"No," she answered limply. "It must be your daughter."

"My daughter?" I asked in confusion. "That makes no sense, witch. I don't have a daughter."

And then the vision that I had just seen came back to me, the small hand plunging the sword into my chest and Raquel's frightened eyes meeting my own as she wept.

I froze, unable to catch a breath as my lungs spasmed uncontrollably and I gasped, trying to draw in air. I felt like a fish out of water as I choked to breathe. And then, just as always when I was overwhelmed, my legs gave out and I tumbled to the ground. I lay there for a moment as Lucan and Hecate rushed to my side. I concentrated on breathing, on trying to absorb what I had just been told.

Visions of Raquel in the Spiritlands and in the courtyard here, assailed me. Her little heart-shaped face and her innocent eyes, her dirty smudged cheeks.

"I don't understand," I whispered. "How can this be? How did I not know?" My hand moved to cup my stomach, where a baby even now grew.

"She is your daughter," Hecate assured me. "It has been hidden from you. I only just now saw it myself. The magic of this place revealed it to me. The Fates kept it carefully concealed." She gestured at the stones around us. "There is powerful magic here."

"But how?..." My hand dropped limply to the ground and I felt weak. "What of the child I am carrying now?" Hecate nodded sadly.

"The child you are carrying now *is* Raquel," she answered simply. "For the Fates' own amusement, they allowed you to become pregnant here in Camelot. When the baby was born, they took it. They allowed her to stay in the palace on Olympus until she grew into a little girl, and then they sent her to Calypso's island, where as you know, time stills. She has remained a child ever since."

"I'm actually pregnant here?" I couldn't wrap my mind around it. "I thought… my mother thought… that I brought the pregnancy with me."

"No," Hecate shook her head. "No. You were pregnant here. You gave birth to the baby before you died in this life and then the Fates took your child while you continued your other cycles as a Keeper."

I shook my head, unable to believe it. "I've had a child all these years and didn't know…"

"To make matters worse," she continued, "The Fates have taunted you with it and you never even knew. They kept her as a child so that they could allow you to come into contact with her in almost every life in some way, only you never knew who she was. It pleased them."

I felt sick. I had missed my daughter's childhood. And while that sickened me to no end, my current predicament came rushing back.

"My daughter must kill me?" My words were like ice, each one frozen on my lips.

Hecate nodded, unable to meet my gaze.

"I cannot do that," I murmured. "To make a child do that… it's just…"

The chieftain stepped forward, his ghostly face glowing beneath the gray clouds.

"You must," he insisted. "It is deplorable, yes. But how many times in history has someone great been forced to do the unthinkable? Many, many times… all for the greater good. You are the chosen one. You must do what others would not do. That is why you were chosen. Do this," he implored. "Do this and allow us to save you. And in doing so, you will save everyone, including your husband and daughter. Don't do it, and everyone will perish."

I wanted to cry. I wanted to rail and scream and bemoan the Fates. But that would not help anything. And every second that I stood here was one more second that they were still in control.

I finally nodded woodenly, my hands clenched into fists at my sides.

"Fine."

Hecate studied my face. "You are certain?"

"Yes," I whispered. "Get her. The king won't notice her absence. They think she is simply an orphaned peasant. Slip in and out and bring her here. But you must tell her what she has to do. I cannot do that."

Hecate nodded and was gone.

I turned to Lucan. "Good knight, I know that this must be perplexing for you. I wish that we had time to explain everything but we do not. Just know that you are a very good man. You have been unfairly persecuted and we will make it right."

He grasped my hand, his grip warm and strong as he stared into my eyes. His gentle brown eyes melted my heart and I fought the urge to cry.

"Are you certain that you want to do this?" he asked. "You will risk so much, my lady."

I looked at him, at his handsome face, and I knew that I would do it a hundred times if need be.

"Yes," I replied firmly. "It is worth it."

Before he could answer, Hecate reappeared with Raquel at her side. Dropping Lucan's hand, I rushed to my daughter. I knew that Hecate wouldn't have told her that I was her mother. That would be cruel given the act that she had to perform. But I could see on her little face that Hecate had told her what she must do. I knelt in front of her, grasping her small hand.

"Do not be afraid," I told her quietly. "You have an important job. We are at war now, and we are all fighting for our lives. You are very important and I appreciate what you will do."

"But my lady," she stammered. "Why must you die? You are so kind."

She was frightened, her hand turning clammy and cold. With goddess hearing, I could hear her little heart racing in her chest and it broke my own.

"There is much you do not yet know, young one," I replied. "And soon, it will be revealed to you. But now, we all must be brave and strong and do what we must. Can you?"

She watched me for a moment, her eyes frightened before she nodded.

"Yes, my lady," she whispered. "I will do anything you wish."

A knot formed in my throat and I could barely swallow it. Raquel had gotten her bravery from her father. She was terrified but she was able to overcome it. She squared her skinny shoulders as I led her to the altar. A sword had appeared on the stone, its blade simple, long and razor sharp. I eyed it calmly. This sword would kill me. Why wasn't I afraid?

I gathered Raquel's hands in my own, kneeling as I looked into her eyes.

"Do not be afraid," I implored her. "I will not really die. I will still be here, just as these men are," and I gestured toward the ghostly warriors surrounding us. "And then, when our battle here has been won, there is much to be explained to you."

As I watched, her blue eyes flickered, replaced for an instant by vivid jade, just like my own. I startled and before I could even comprehend what I had seen, they had changed back to blue.

Realization settled upon me. The Fates had altered her appearance, making sure she was disguised during all of these millennia. I would have recognized her eyes. My anger fueled me and I climbed onto the stone, lying back onto the cold surface.

"It is time," I told Raquel. "Don't be afraid. Just pick up the sword and let us get this done."

I watched as her little hands grasped the handle of the sword and she tentatively approached me. She was terrified.

"It will be alright," I assured her. "I promise."

She nodded and raised the sword directly over my chest. I could practically see her heart beating in hers, it was pounding so hard. The blade glistened in the light, the tip a mere foot from my body, just as in my vision.

"Do it," I whispered. "Just do it, child."

The blade descended as Lucan cried, "NO!" from the perimeter of the circle.

But it was too late. The sword sliced cleanly into my chest, cutting through clothing and flesh and bone, embedding into my heart. I felt my heart stutter one time and then still, as my vision turned cloudy and then faded to inky black.

And then suddenly, I was standing next to the chieftain, watching Raquel weep as her body was bathed in my blood.

"Raquel," I said quietly, grasping her arm.

She turned and gasped. I knew I must appear as the warriors, slightly transparent and glowing. She looked from me to my inert body lying in a pool of blood on the stone. I could feel Lucan and Hecate watching me, as well. The meadow was silent, the air charged with what had just transpired.

In all honesty, I didn't feel any differently. My hand on Raquel's arm felt firm and solid, as though I was flesh and blood. My feet were planted firmly in the soil, my hair was rustling in the wind. The only difference was that my heart didn't beat in my chest.

"It is alright," I assured everyone.

Hecate nodded knowingly. She was accustomed to supernatural things and this did not surprise her. Lucan was astounded, but as always, he handled himself with strength, standing stoically behind me. My daughter launched herself at my legs, weeping.

"My lady, I'm so sorry," she cried. "I didn't want to do it. I really didn't."

I picked her up and leaned my forehead into hers.

"Raquel, do you feel that? Do you feel me? I am here with you and I am fine. You had an important job to do and you did it. I am very proud of you. And when this is over, you will be rewarded."

She looked up at me, her pink lip quivering. "Truly? You will truly be fine?"

I nodded. "I promise. I will truly be fine." And honestly, as I studied the group of chieftains surrounding me, seeing how their numbers extended well into the surrounding field, spilling over the crest of the hilltop, I believed it for the first time.

"Everything will be fine," I told her again as I straightened up and picked up the black box of souls. Glancing up, the red-headed chieftain caught my eye and he nodded.

I sat the box down in the middle of the stone and climbed up next to it, stepping over my lifeless mortal body, treading through my own blood. Bending, I pulled the sword out of my chest, listening to the moist sound it made as it slid from my mortal wound.

Somehow, it didn't bother me. I wasn't sure if it was bravery or numbness that fueled me now, but I was not afraid. Gripping the handle, I plunged it into the box, watching as it split in two. Thousands of shrieks filled the sky around me as souls poured from the box.

One by one, I watched the displaced souls find their bodies. One by one, I watched the warriors surrounding me return to life, taking deep breaths as their mortal lungs once again filled with air.

It was an amazing sight. Lucan, Hecate, Raquel and I stood quietly as the warriors crowded around us. And then I grew weak. My legs felt as though they would give out as my fingers turned cold and numb. I started to say something, to ask what was happening, when I was suddenly gasping for air on the stone altar.

Staring around me in bewilderment, I realized that I had been thrust back into my mortal body. My wound had closed, although blood still surrounded me. Looking down, I found my green dress blood-stained and torn where the sword had entered my chest, but I was alive once more.

"What… How…" I couldn't form a cohesive sentence.

The red-headed chieftain smiled down at me, reaching down to grasp my hand and helped me to stand.

"Your first act as the Chosen One," he explained, "Was to exhibit faith. You died so that others would live. You gave the ultimate sacrifice because you had faith and in doing so, you have proven yourself worthy."

He leaped to the stone, looking around at the warriors.

"Take a knee!" he cried. Every one of the warriors dropped to one knee, bowing their heads in deference.

"As many of you have given fealty to me, and have also taken fealty from others, so too will you offer your allegiance to the goddess Harmonia now."

Murmurings of assent filled the meadow.

Cries of "We ride with you, Harmonia!" and "I vow my allegiance to you!" filled my ears and I stared around me in disbelief. Throughout time, in every life, I had assisted royalty and served them as I fulfilled the plans of Fate. Now, as we stood on this precipice of saving all that we knew, I would command a legion. It seemed incredible.

I stepped forward and held up a hand, quieting the crowd.

"I am honored to ride with you," I began and they erupted into cheers once more. I waited a moment for them to quiet and continued. "Together, we will save Camelot and everything that we know!"

In the magnitude of the moment, I bowed my head and stood in the sun. The most important time of my life was still to come and there was nothing left to do but embrace it.

CHAPTER EIGHTEEN

"Harmonia?" a familiar voice called and I startled at the recognition in Lucan's voice. He was pushing through the crowd to stand at the base of the stone, familiarity written all over him as he stared up at me.

"Lucan?" I asked, too afraid to hope. But Cadmus' soul had been in the box. When I released the souls, of course it had nowhere to go, but to where it belonged- in Lucan's body.

"Cadmus?" I asked uncertainly.

Lucan leaped to stand next to me in one bound and pulled me into a fierce embrace, pushing my hair out of the way as he bent to kiss my lips. Cheers once again erupted, but I ignored them

"I am here, my sweet," he assured me as he clutched me close. "My body is still in the Spiritlands, but I am here with you now. I am so proud of you, although I want to throttle you at the same time for taking this chance."

I stared into his chocolate eyes, so beautiful and familiar to me.

"This was not a chance," I told him firmly. "Without you, I'm not alive at all."

He pulled me close once more and I rested for just a moment against his strength, breathing him in, happier than I would've thought possible. It didn't matter that we were about to face a battle of epic proportions. We were going to do it together.

Helping me down from the altar, he pulled Hecate into a hug, as well. "Thank you, witch," he smiled. "For everything you've done."

"It isn't over yet," she reminded him, but her eyes were twinkling as she clasped his arm.

He knelt at Raquel's feet and I watched him study her small face. He took her hand and kissed it.

"Thank you, young one, for your bravery," he told her solemnly. "When this is over, we shall have a long conversation. There are many things that you should know."

Raquel nodded and he kept her hand in his as he turned to face me once more.

"We have a battalion now," he observed. "But no horses. Hecate?"

"Taken care of," she answered and as we watched, enough war horses to equip an entire battalion appeared in the open field next to us. They stamped their feet and tossed their heads, anxious to do battle. I shook my head. Was there nothing Hecate couldn't do?

"Mount up!" the chieftain yelled. "We ride!"

The warriors charged for the field, each choosing a horse and within minutes, everyone was mounted and ready to travel. Cadmus lifted Raquel onto the saddle of his horse and then swung around behind her.

My own horse pranced next to his and I climbed astride her.

"Are you ready?" he grinned.

"Ready," I answered.

We took off across the dead grasses of the Camelot plains. We still had a sword to find. The sheer number of our battalion caused our horses' hooves to sound like thunder, booming across the land as our horses ran. Minutes once again turned into an hour and then two as we galloped across the browned fields.

From time to time, I glanced over at Lucan and Raquel and found her leaning comfortably against him. It warmed my heart in ways I had never known. I had been a wife, a daughter and a friend for thousands of years. But now I would be a mother. I had a family of my own. Even in the midst of this chaos and fear, it was enough to give me hope.

The long ride extended longer and longer and finally, when I was growing very weary of riding, buildings rose from the horizon and I sighed in relief. Dying and coming back to life had taken my energy.

"We're almost there," Hecate called from behind us.

I spurred my horse faster, with Lucan and Hecate directly on my flanks. A few minutes later, we rode into a compound of buildings, surrounded by a stone fence. The gates were standing open, so we passed easily beneath.

A large cobblestone house stood within the fence, with large barns behind it. This did not appear like the kind of home that the parents of a king would live in, but his foster parents had not been flashy. Merlin had brought baby Arthur here when he was just an infant, arranging for Sir Ector, a wealthy farmer, and his wife to raise Arthur as their own.

And they had. Arthur had grown up thinking that they were his loving parents and he ran the hills with his brother, Kay. As the second son, he had been the lovable carefree spirit in the family.

Kay, being the eldest, was left to be responsible. But that all changed when Arthur's real father, King Uther, died and Merlin returned to claim Arthur. Until that day, Arthur had had no inkling that he was the son of a king. He left his foster parents and traveled to Camelot with Merlin and Kay. And he was meant to change history. But he was meant to change history with his compassion and grace, not by becoming heartless and cruel.

I shook my head. I couldn't focus on the travesty of it all right now. I needed to find the sword. The balance of the world hinged upon it.

Riding through the short wrought-iron gates, I glanced around. The yard in front of the house was crunchy and dead. Withered flower beds lined the front of the house, although the home itself was immaculately kept. Clearly, Arthur was paying someone to care for it and the grounds. It was neat and clean, although it was stark and clearly empty. There was nothing for miles around us, no signs of life. It was completely desolate.

"No one appears to be home," Cadmus observed as he drew up next to me.

"That's good," I smiled. "The inhabitants are dead, so I certainly prefer it that way."

He shot me an amused look, but stayed silent and urged his horse ahead, before dropping to the ground and looking around. Hecate sidled up next to me and we lifted Raquel down from her horse before tying the horses to a hitching post.

My body was screaming, my arms aching, but there was no time to rest. For all we knew, Arthur had sent a party of knights to follow us. We just couldn't take that chance. Leaving our army standing behind us, we moved toward the house.

Walking softly up the front porch steps, I tested the door. It was locked. Quickly, I crushed the brass door handle in my hand. It fell to the ground in bits and pieces. The door opened easily now.

Walking inside, I stopped in the foyer and spun in a slow circle. The house was as neat as a pin. With the land outside reduced to rubble, it seemed strange to find this house still in perfect condition. It made me believe that somewhere, deep down, Arthur retained some of his true characteristics. Why else would he care so much for his deceased parents' home?

The silence was chilling. Walking through a dining room, I observed a long table with crystal centerpieces and a long bench on each side. There was space for at least twelve. It seemed strange to find a place that I was sure once bustled with life and laughter, so empty now. Every footstep echoed loudly throughout the house as I made my way upstairs.

It didn't seem plausible that Arthur would have hidden the sword in the house where anyone could find it, but I had to look. It made no sense not to. So, I combed quickly through every room. And in every room, I turned up nothing but everyday household items. There was no sword here.

As I entered the last room at the end of a narrow hall, I felt an even eerier stillness descend upon me and I stopped moving and glanced around.

It was simply a bedroom. A large bedroom, one that might once have been airy and light, back when the sun still shone brightly. Now, however, it was dismal and cold. The heavy draperies were pulled tightly closed and the dark red velvet bedclothes sucked any semblance of light from the room.

Sliding my fingers along a long armoire, I found that there was not a trace of dust. Someone was caring for this farm house. I picked up a silver hairbrush. It was polished to a gleam, no sign of tarnish. Yet no one lived here. It was so curious that Arthur would go to this trouble.

I glanced into the heavy, ornate mirror that hung above the armoire. I looked tired. My face was pale and dark circles lined my green eyes. I lifted a hand and brushed my hair away from my face, tucking it behind my ear with a sigh. I was certainly not at my best.

And suddenly, I was not alone.

In the mirror, Morgan appeared behind me, her face stark and white. Her dark eyes seemed sunken and severe and I spun around quickly. She wasn't behind me. I slowly turned back around, facing her once more. *She was in the mirror.*

"What is this?" I hissed, backing away from it. "What are you doing?"

She smiled, not maliciously, but not a friendly grin, either. She was simply amused. Her dark gowns only emphasized her severe look, making her face seem even paler. It occurred to me that she didn't look well, either. Exhaustion was apparent on her face.

"Did I frighten you?" she asked. "That was not my intention. I cast a wide spell so that the next time you looked into your reflection, I could find you. I did not mean to frighten you."

"Of course you did," I snapped. "You know you did."

"Oh, Harmonia," she sighed. "So many things have changed and you don't even realize it."

"What?" I unconsciously lifted my hand to my throat. "You called me Harmonia."

"Of course I did," she sniffed. "Isn't that your name? What do you take me for?"

"Morgan le Fey, sister of the king," I answered uncertainly. Did she also know who she was? She answered my question with her next breath.

"That is who I appear as, true," she acknowledged. "But you and I both know the truth, don't we? We are not mortals, you and I. Is Hecate with you?"

"What is going on?" I asked uncertainly. "How do you know these things?"

And further troubling, she was not herself. Eris was not being malicious. And that was unusual and frightening in itself.

"Ahmose came to me," she explained finally. "He showed me who I am and what the Fates did to me in the future. I am of a mind to work with you for the time being."

"Work with me?" My eyebrow shot up. "Really?" I couldn't keep the doubt from my voice and she smiled again.

"Yes, really," she confirmed and with that, she stepped from the mirror onto the armoire and then jumped lightly to stand next to me. I didn't even flinch. "Apparently, you are the chosen one of some sort and if I have any hopes of surviving this intact, I will work with you, not against you."

"What do you propose?" I asked suspiciously. There was no way I was trusting this woman, even if Ahmose did. No way in hell.

She narrowed her eyes. "First, I propose that we find the sword. You're not having much luck on your own, are you? Let us find Hecate and together, we shall summon it."

I stared at her blankly as she gripped my elbow and led me toward the door. My feet stubbornly lagged behind because old habits died hard. I didn't want to go anywhere with her, but I reluctantly accompanied her to the main floor where we found Cadmus and Hecate. Cadmus was startled when I appeared with another person in the doorway, but Hecate only seemed expectant. There was not a trace of surprise on her face. I glared at her.

"Let me guess," I snapped. "You knew this already?"

She nodded. "I did see it in my dreams last eve."

"It was a long ride here, with plenty of time for you to have shared that. A little forewarning would have been nice," I replied.

"I'll try to remember that for next time," she grinned. I rolled my eyes at her and turned to Morgan.

"You'll have to excuse my reluctance to trust you," I said cautiously. "We've been at odds for a long time and you have wronged me again and again. I'm finding it difficult to believe you now."

"So, all the better to end that, correct?" she asked me with her eyebrows raised into her hairline. "There is no time like the present. In fact, if we do not, there may not be time left for anything at all. You know that I always act in my own best interest. Acting against the Fates is in my best interest. I know that now, thanks to Ahmose."

"Morgan," Cadmus said, "Isn't the king wondering where you are?"

"No," she answered. "The king is still at the palace. Much has changed there. I'm here on my own volition…to help."

"Really?" Cadmus asked. "Isn't that treasonous to your king… your brother?"

Eris barely spared him a glance.

"There is much you do not know, knight," she said as she stepped forward. "And I do not have time to explain. Hecate, I will require your assistance. Together, perhaps we can see the sword. I have learned a few tricks as Morgan."

Hecate's face was impassive as she stepped beside my ancient adversary.

"Where do you want to do this?" she asked quietly.

"The barn would be best, I think," Morgan replied. She turned and began walking through the house, her back ramrod straight.

"You can't be serious," I implored Hecate. "There's no way that this can be real. I cannot trust that woman."

"You must," Hecate insisted. "Ahmose has sent her to you. I know that you must trust him. He has willingly died to protect you. That should speak for something."

I considered that guiltily. Of course it did. He must know things that I did not, the absolute story of my life. I took a deep breath and followed the two women, with Cadmus and little Raquel close on my heels.

They led us out to the abandoned barn. The inside was dark and cold and I could hear the scurrying of small mice from the corners. An owl hooted quietly from the rafters and I fought the urge to turn and run out. Something did not feel right about this place. It was too still, too silent.

Eris snapped her fingers and blazing torches appeared in every corner, spreading warm light throughout the room. Cadmus inhaled sharply behind me, but still he remained silent.

"Come forward," Hecate directed as she and Eris waited for us to approach. "Closer."

We stepped forward and at Hecate's gesture, we moved to stand in line with them. Hecate began muttering beneath her breath and Eris joined in, both of them fixated on the ground in front of them. I looked, but there was nothing there other than the stone floor. Unconsciously, I fingered my bloodstone. It was practically vibrating. I yanked my fingers away and my gaze flew to Hecate and Eris. Their eyes were closed now as they chanted.

Cadmus looked at me. "What is happening?" He sounded nervous for the first time.

"I do not know," I answered him truthfully. "But I think we will find out soon." I glanced at Raquel. "Don't worry, little one. Everything will be fine."

Their chanting got louder and boards began flying from the rafters, crashing down around us. I jumped, but stood firmly in place as the women continued to chant. Eris threw her arms in the air and the roof of the barn lifted off and flew to the side, taking with it pieces of the walls. Bit by bit, the remaining walls followed until we were standing in the open air, next to a large pile of rubble.

And then, with an alarming wrenching split, the earth in front of us opened up, throwing stones away from the floor. Cadmus grasped my elbow and pulled me slightly away, protective as ever. I kept my eyes on the churning mess in front of us because I knew it wasn't over yet.

A giant hole formed in front of us, jagged and deep. And then before I could even process that, it filled with water. I couldn't see where the water came from... it was most likely summoned from the earth itself. The pit filled, churning and rocking. The moisture from the water splattered onto me in droplets and I licked it from my lips.

And then everything was still.

I tensed in anticipation as Hecate and Eris stared pointedly at the water, clearly waiting for something to happen. Cadmus' grip on my arm tightened as we kept our eyes trained on the newly formed pond.

And then ripples began bubbling from the center. I craned forward, anxious to see what would emerge. What could they have summoned here? What could possibly help us?

As I held my breath, a woman slowly rose from the water, her head down and her long blonde hair dripping all around her as she walked toward me. Her white cotton dress was completely sheer in its current soaked state. She might as well have been naked.

She raised her head and met my gaze, her eyes shiny. She was ethereal, seemingly radiating light from within. Her skin was oh-so-pale, her lips a natural pink. I knew her.

"Thalassa," I murmured in surprise. She was a sea goddess, the daughter of Hemera.

"They refer to me as the Lady of the Lake here," she replied softly, the corners of her mouth curved slightly. "Hello, Harmonia."

"Hello," I answered hesitantly, subconsciously moving closer to Cadmus.

"Aren't you glad to see me?" she laughed. "I come bearing gifts."

And then I noticed... a large sword dangled from one hand.

CHAPTER NINETEEN

Zeus' sword, the one thing that could save everything, was directly in front of me. I took one step forward and Thalassa took one step back. She cocked her head as I looked at her questioningly.

"Are you not here to give me the sword?" I was confused by her behavior.

She nodded. "I want to. But I was entrusted with the care of this sword by Arthur himself. He gave it to me in exchange when I gave him Excalibur. He took my word that I would never surrender it to anyone but him. And the only way I can do so now is to see proof that you are indeed the Chosen One."

"Proof?" I stared at her in bewilderment, before I turned my wrist over and thrust it toward her. "I am marked. See?"

She glanced at the bird-shaped mark on my pulsepoint. "I see. But that is not enough."

"Then what do you desire?" I asked impatiently. "We are wasting time here."

She faced me patiently. "Harmonia, Ahmose came to me yesterday and explained who you are and why you need this sword. He also said that you would find me and that when you did, you would be happy to provide me with proof. Surely you understand, I gave my oath to someone. I am bound by that. I cannot simply break it without good cause."

I nodded slowly, letting a thin rush of air exhale over my teeth as I thought.

As my mind spun in circles, I absently glanced around me at the demolished barn. The wood and stone stood in jagged shambles around us, pieces scattered at our feet. The stone foundation still stood intact, a perfect box around us. The barn owl, displaced when the building flew apart, fluttered to a rest on the edge of the foundation. He blinked his round golden eyes at me.

A bird. I fingered my birth mark as an idea came to me.

I could control the phoenix. I had done it only once before and I had been overwhelmingly afraid at the time, ruled by instinct. But surely I could do it again. I closed my eyes, keeping my fingers on my birthmark.

Concentrating, I felt my blood pulse through my veins, every beat of my heart pushing beneath the bird on my wrist. I focused, allowing every emotion inside of me to rise to the surface, pulsing against me.

The people standing with me faded away, the demolished barn slipping from my sight. All I could see was a blend of colors as everything swirled together and I closed my eyes.

My blood turned warm and then warmer, pulsing faster and faster as my heart beat increased. Finally, I was hot, my cheeks flushed as I conjured every emotion I could think of, focusing only on the image of the Phoenix.

And then it came.

I knew from the gasps of those standing behind me and I opened my eyes.

Flying from the distance, it was vivid and bright as its feathers burned in the sky. Orange, red and amber, it was a ball of flame as it descended upon us. His eyes were brilliant azure and they focused first on me and then on Thalassa with razor precision. Swooping down low from the sky, it spread its fiery wings in a wide span as it glided in from the clouds above us. It was a magnificent sight as it trailed fire in its wake like a comet.

I felt its intense heat as it dove in front of me, scooping up the sword from Thalassa's grasp. With a shrill cry, it looped around above us and circled back, dipping once more in front of me as it dropped the sword at my feet. I watched it roll to a stop mere inches from my toes, before I looked again to the phoenix.

He flew to a stop on the far end of the barn's foundation. As I watched, his flame died down to nothing and he stopped burning. His feathers were shiny and crimson, iridescent in the light. His brilliant gaze was trained on me and I dipped my head in thanks. He returned the gesture and I turned my attention once more to Thalassa.

"Is that proof enough?" I asked drily.

She nodded, impressed and shocked.

"The sword is yours," she replied simply. "Use it well."

I bent to examine it. It wasn't that impressive, to be honest. It was plain, with a simple bone handle. The blade was long and thin, and although it was sharp, it wasn't shiny. It was free of any jewels or embellishments…it was just a simple sword.

But it was oh-so- important.

I picked it up and a current of electricity moved through my arms. This was definitely the sword. I ran my fingers lightly along the blade. It seemed strange that something so normal carried with it so much weight. I shifted my gaze to Thalassa.

"You had to know that this wasn't a normal sword when Arthur gave it to you," I raised my eyebrow.

"I did," she acknowledged. "But I had no way of knowing what exactly it was. I thought it was simply something that Merlin had conjured. But it wasn't until he came to me yesterday that I knew it for exactly what it was."

"So Merlin knew what it was? Did he always know?" I asked in shock.

She nodded. "Yes. I believe that is why he arranged to have Arthur bring it to me in the first place. It was he who suggested to Arthur that I keep it safe for him. And now that Arthur is... not himself, it clearly should be used by you to set things right."

"Thank you," I uttered quickly, remembering my manners. "You have no idea how important this is. I appreciate your kindness. I don't really understand the part that you play in all of this, Thalassa, but I do thank you."

"Oh, my part is fairly simple," she sighed. "Once, long ago, I became smitten with Merlin, or Ahmose as you call him. I swore to him that I would help him in any way that I could if he should ever need me. When the Fates assigned him to Camelot, he needed me here.

"I created Excalibur and enchanted it for Arthur's use in battle. And truthfully, I did not mind. I grew to respect young King Arthur. A purer soul or gentler spirit I have never seen. To think of him as they tell me that he is now is heartbreaking. Don't you agree?"

Her lovely face was pained and she didn't wait for me to respond before she continued.

"Merlin continued to visit me during his life here. The mortals here created the tale of the Lady of the Lake to explain things away to their satisfaction. I have been Arthur's guardian, so to speak. I hesitate to hand the privilege to you, but Merlin has told me that I can trust you, that you are strong and brave."

"Merlin is kind to me," I replied. "I hope that I can measure up to his expectations."

"If you do not, he will die," Thalassa stated quietly. "And I feel as though he is the very air that I breathe. I do not wish to lose him. He has more wisdom in one finger than most of the gods on Olympus put together. You must save him."

I nodded. "I will try, Thalassa. Trust me on that."

Someone rustled nervously behind me, bringing my attention back to the present. I stared at Thalassa's pale, calm face, ethereal in her beauty and made a decision. I had to keep Raquel safe. And I didn't have many options right now.

"Thalassa, I have a request."

I felt everyone's eyes upon me, wondering what I was going to ask at this particular juncture. Thalassa had, after all, just given us what we needed.

"Can you keep this child with you for now, so that she stays safe during the battle that is coming? I wish no harm to come to her."

Thalassa nodded thoughtfully, her blonde hair drying as we spoke. She lifted a pale hand and brushed it away from her face.

"Of course, Harmonia. I shall keep her under the lake with me. She will be safe, I assure you. My underwater world is protected by enchantment. No one may enter without my permission, not even the Fates."

I turned, motioning Raquel to the front. Kneeling in front of her, I grasped her hands. I started to tell her to go with Thalassa, but hesitated at the frightened look on her small face.

"Raquel, I must tell you something." I glanced up at Cadmus and he quickly joined me, kneeling next to us on one knee. He reached out and grasped my hand.

"This might be hard for you to hear and we will discuss it more later, but I need you to know something before you go." She waited expectantly, playing restlessly with her fingers.

"You are mine," I whispered.

"Yours?" she repeated, confusion apparent on her face and in her voice. "I don't understand."

"You are mine. And Lucan's. We aren't what you think. Our names are really Harmonia and Cadmus and we live in a beautiful place called the Spiritlands. You were taken from us long ago by wretched old women. I'm so sorry that you found out in this way, but I wanted you to know."

She stared at me seriously. "I am not an orphan? You're my mother, my lady?"

I nodded. "And when this is over, we will be a family and we will be so happy together. I promise."

Cadmus spoke up. "I have never seen a prettier little girl. You must get your beauty from your mother."

Raquel shifted her gaze to him and reached out with a shaking little hand, placing it on Cadmus' cheek.

"Can I call you papa?" she whispered.

Cadmus took a sharp breath and his eyes grew watery. I squeezed his hand.

"Of course you can, little one," he answered softly, drawing her into his arms. "And I will work hard to make you the happiest little girl in the world when we return." He held her for a few minutes longer and then released her. She stepped back. As I stared at her, I had the sudden need to see her true appearance.

"Hecate?" I turned. "Can you reveal her true face? I know that the Fates disguised her. Can you show her to me?"

Hecate stepped forward and placed her hands on Raquel's shoulders. She murmured for a moment, her body blocking Raquel from my sight. I waited anxiously, gripping Cadmus' hand. Yes, I knew that we had important things to be doing, but to me, this was the most important thing of all in this moment.

Hecate finally stepped away and there was a collective gasp from everyone.

She looked just like me.

Her skin was a golden tan, her hair dark. She did have her father's chin, but her eyes were mine. Vivid jade green, they sparkled as she stared at us. I could clearly see why the Fates had disguised her. There is no way that I wouldn't have known who she was otherwise.

"Is something wrong?" she asked worriedly, her hand unconsciously moving to her throat.

"No, little one," I answered softly, moving to hug her. "You just look different. That's all."

Guiding her shoulders, I led her to the water's edge where she could see her reflection. When she looked down, she gasped as well.

"I look like you!" she exclaimed, moving her hand to touch her cheeks, her hair, her shoulders. "Just like you."

"Yes," I agreed. "You do. Because you're my daughter." I would never get tired of saying the words. Gripping her skinny shoulders, I turned her to face me.

"Go with Thalassa," I instructed. "When this is over, we will return for you."

She nodded obediently. "You'll come back for me?" she asked worriedly.

"Of course we will," I assured her. "Just as soon as this is over and it is safe once again." She nodded trustingly and took Thalassa's outstretched hand.

"This will be fun," Thalassa promised her with a smile. "Do you like flowers and sea sprites?" Raquel was staring at her in wonder as they submerged into the water and disappeared. A couple of ripples spanned the pool before it went still.

I looked at Hecate and Lucan, taking a deep breath.

"What now?"

Hecate nibbled her lip thoughtfully. "Much has happened over the past couple of days," she said. "While the Fates have changed so much, there are some things that have stayed just the same. Look."

She gestured toward the water and a picture formed on the still surface. There was a banquet in the castle and Mordred was somehow seated at Arthur's right in Lancelot's normal seat. Arthur was wearing an icy, dark expression, something I had never seen on his face before. He looked cruel, just as my mother had said. My heart sank in my chest.

I watched Mordred whisper something in the king's ear and Arthur's face clouded over. Leaping to his feet, his stormed through the mass of people from the room and down a hall. In a dark corner, Lancelot and Guinevere were sequestered, with Lancelot's mouth by her ear. I didn't know what they were doing, but it certainly looked compromising. Arthur rose up in front of them like an avenging, angry god.

"What is this?" King Arthur boomed.

Lancelot jumped away from my mother, but I noticed that he kept her safely behind him. He returned Arthur's stare without flinching, clearly unafraid, even though he still showed respect.

"Nothing, your highness," Lancelot answered loudly. "It isn't what it seems."

"Then explain to me what it is!" King Arthur's voice was sharp enough to cut glass. "Do you know the penalty for treason? And consorting with the king's wife is most certainly treason in the highest form."

"Arthur, truly it isn't..." Guinevere began, but the king cut her off.

"Be silent!" he roared. "You think to humiliate me in front of my people? You are condemned to death, woman. You can ponder your sins in isolation today. Your crown is stripped from you. You will burn at dawn."

He spun on his heel and whirled around, his cloak swirling.

"Throw them in the dungeons!" he called over his shoulder as he climbed the stairs to his quarters. There was not an ounce of emotion in his voice, but for rage. This was not the Arthur that I knew.

Mordred and Gawain stepped forward and restrained Lancelot, their faces impassive and cold. I expected that from Mordred, because he had clearly orchestrated this little revealing incident. But Gawain. This was unlike him, as well.

Percivale and Gaheris took the queen's arms, pulling her with them down the long halls to the dungeons. To their credit, my parents allowed themselves to be taken prisoner, even though they could easily have escaped. They disappeared down the hall.

"Where are they now?" I whispered.

The water rippled and another picture formed. Guinevere was hanging in a dungeon, exactly how we had found Cadmus. She was not bloodied, but she was hanging limply, her eyes closed. Her hands were white from loss of blood as they were bound tightly above her head. Lancelot was in the oubliette, staring ferociously at the dark wall. He was stripped of his shirt and there were lash-marks on his back. They had beaten him and he had allowed it. Pride surged through me at the determination of my parents.

They were sacrificing everything for this and now they were waiting for me.

"Mother, it is time," I whispered. Her eyes snapped open, turning silver at my words. My father raised his head, his dark eyes meeting mine through the darkness.

It is time, I repeated silently.

They were gone. Both disappeared in the blink of an eye, my mother's manacles dangling limply in the air where she had just been hanging.

"Well, that certainly took you long enough," my father growled from behind me.

I turned just in time for my mother to rush into my arms.

"Are you alright?" she asked anxiously. "Why are you bloody?" She held me at arm's length examining me.

"I'm fine now," I answered. "I'm happy that you're here and I'm sorry for the delay. But we have the sword."

My father clapped me on the back.

"Well done, daughter," he said approvingly. "I knew you would do it." He was sweaty and bloody, but he didn't appear to mind. The lashes on his back were deep, but he didn't even flinch as he moved. My father had the strength of an ox and he was almost just that big.

Cadmus stepped forward. "Ares," he dipped his head. "Aphrodite."

They stared at him as if he had two heads. I smiled.

"Lucan knows everything. I opened the box of souls and Cadmus' soul is now in this body. It's a long story."

"One that I will be interested in hearing," my mother replied, her eyebrow raised.

Hecate interrupted, her voice firm.

"And you will. But not right now. We have a battle to wage."

CHAPTER TWENTY

Hecate looked seriously at me, then at Cadmus and my parents.

"Let us rejoin the others. We must form a strategy."

Taking my arm, my mother walked with me, as the others lagged behind. She didn't seem bothered at all by the fact that she has just been hanging in chains, something that I found strange. She casually remarked about the desolation of the countryside and the quiet plains surrounding us which caused me to stare at her with my mouth open.

"Are you alright, mother?" I asked. "You seem strangely unbothered by all that has happened."

She turned her silvery gaze upon me.

"Why? Because I am not weeping? I am choosing not to think of it, for fear that I would not be able to control my anger. You know my temper, dear one. If I knew what had happened to cause your injuries," and she gestured at my bloody clothing, "Or if I focused on the satisfied look that sniveling Mordred had when he ordered me into chains, then I fear that my temper would rage. And that would not behoove us. Instead, let us prepare for vengeance, yes?"

She was eerily calm and I had to admire her effort. I knew though, that all hell would break loose at some point. Her calm façade would crack and then she would explode.

The battalion of undead chieftains was still converged on the field next to the old farmhouse. Their horses were calm and they were all still, patiently waiting for us to reappear.

They were already lined up in battle formations and I smiled at their enthusiasm.

My mother startled as she saw their vast number, and then she quickly regained her composure like the goddess that she was. She didn't even ask any questions. She simply took her place quietly at the front of the crowd next to me, as we waited for Hecate, Cadmus and Ares, who were just a few steps behind us.

Hecate stepped forward and addressed them.

"In the past, as gods from the Spiritlands, any time that we have traveled in the mortal world, it has always been necessary to leave things as we found them, to not interfere. But now, today, that is no longer a problem. The Fates have changed things so completely, that we cannot do any further harm. We have raised a battalion of the finest Briton warriors from the dead and we shall call upon every available resident in the Spiritlands to help us this day."

There were a few shouts of approval as she closed her eyes and murmured, her voice raising to a chant. Every eye in the crowd was trained on her, waiting to see who she would summon. Even the horses were still in anticipation.

And suddenly, the empty field to our left was filled. Ortrera and her warriors were in the front, sitting atop their massive warhorses. Their huge wings rose and fell softly as they breathed. Behind them were various gods and goddesses from the Spiritlands, all armed and wearing ferocious expressions. I could see Chaos, Erythia, Hypnos and Iris leading the mass of familiar faces. Aeolus, the god of the wind, leaned forward in his saddle and winked at me. I nodded my head toward him. He might come in handy here. Everyone, it seemed, was ready to fight.

Ares stepped from behind me to the front, his bulging muscles glistening in the light, his torso still bare. As I watched, his expression transformed into that of a warrior, into the god of war, and my stomach trembled at the sight in front of me. This was the sight that so many had seen as they drew their last breaths... as my father had taken their lives from them.

His abs were ripped and tight, his arms as hard as steel. His eyes were deadly and I shivered slightly as his gaze passed over me and examined the crowd.

"Today," Ares shouted, "Every one of you here is a warrior. We fight for one common cause- to restore the world to what it should be. The mortal world and my own have been overturned by the whims of the twisted.

"Today," he continued, "We will rise above it and take it back. On our backs, we will carry truth and righteousness. We will be armed with honor and dignity."

The crowd erupted into shouts and cheers. Ares stood proudly, enormous and frightening, as the people yelled. Finally, he gestured for silence and the noise died down quickly as everyone awaited his next words.

"I am the god of war!" he shouted to more cheers. "And I am honored to have you in my army. Follow me this day and we will emerge victorious!"

He raised his huge fist in the air and the crowd exploded into screams. He swaggered back to his place in line, grinning cockily at me as he did.

Hecate stepped forward once more, her expression severe.

"The Fates will not fight with honor," she warned and the crowd reacted with jeers.

"They cannot fight with honor, because they have none!" someone yelled and Hecate nodded.

"You are correct," she shouted. "They have no honor. You must expect the unexpected because that is what you will receive.   The Fates will use your fears against you, so endeavor to have none.   They will exploit every weakness, every hesitation against us. Do not give them that chance. If we fail today, all will be lost. So fight today as if there is no tomorrow, because if we lose, there will not be."

She pivoted, scanning the crowd, meeting the gaze of many of the warriors.

"I am the goddess of witchcraft," she shouted. "I will enchant your horses and offer incantations to protect you. But for every spell I use, the Fates will have one also. Our victory today will come down to the pure hearts of the righteous and my friends, that advantage belongs to us!"

Once more, the ground trembled from the shouts and stomps of the legions in front of us.   Cadmus glanced sideways at me and reached out to grasp my hand.   I squeezed his fingers.   Oddly, as we balanced on this precarious place, on the brink of winning everything or losing the same, I wasn't afraid. I was deadly calm and ready to move.

"I wish for my son to not be harmed!" someone shouted and everyone craned their necks to see who had spoken. A man, broad-shouldered and dressed in a lavish fur cloak pushed through the throngs of people to the front. His dark-blonde hair was long and curly, his eyes ferocious and cornflower blue. He wore a glittering crown.

King Uther Pendragon.

I sucked in a breath. I hadn't realized that he was among the assembled warriors, although I should have guessed. His cunning in battle was talked about still, his intelligence and lack of mercy for those who offended him. He was very different from his son, yet they shared the same blood.

He turned to address the crowd.

"My son is not truly the person whom you will see today," he said, his voice booming loud enough to reach the warriors standing in the very last row. "The Fates have manipulated him and turned him into something that he is not. Do not shed his blood if you can help it. He is a true king."

The mounted warriors nodded in affirmation. Everyone knew of Arthur's plight, of the goodness that he used to embody. Tales of he and his knights had spread through the kingdom like wildfire from the moment that he had assumed the crown.

Hecate once again stepped forward and stood shoulder to shoulder with King Uther.

"To ensure that our fight is as equally matched as possible, we will need to draw on some rather unlikely resources. As you may know, I hold the keys to the underworld. Today, I will open the gates and we will bring with us horrific beasts to help us in our fight."

There were murmurings and whispers. The warriors moved restlessly, trying to keep their horses still, but even the horses felt the tension here and it made them nervous. Hecate ignored everything and focused on the ground. I gritted my teeth in anticipation. We would do what we had to do using whatever methods necessary, but it didn't mean that I had to enjoy it.

Before I could think another thought, the ground in front of me opened, a yawning, black hole and haunting screams emitted from it. Full of fear and pain, the howls reached our ears, filling our hearts with dread. It was the sound of the underworld.

The warriors in the front automatically backed away from the sound and I couldn't blame them. I wanted to do the same, but I stood fast, gripping Cadmus' fingers tightly.

A horrific thunder shook the land around us as a metallic rattle echoed from the hole. The heavy sounds grew nearer and within seconds, a team of massive metal horses screamed from the tunnel, screeching to a stop in front of Hecate.

Their bronze sides heaved as their nostrils flared with flame, their front hooves slamming against the ground in agitation. They were ferocious and strong and I knew them. My step-father, Hephaestus had created them, breathing fire into their throats himself. These were the Horses of the Cabiri. Crafted from bronze, they had crimson red eyes and could breathe fire and withstand any injury. Their hearts were as black as night. They tossed their heads impatiently as they stood.

"Uther!" Hecate called. "You may drive this team of demons."

Uther stepped forward without hesitation to claim their reigns, stepping onto the empty golden chariot that they pulled. He raced with them to the back of the crowd where he turned them and fell into place within the ranks.

A coldness descended upon us and I glanced furtively around. Black mist seeped from the tunnel and I leaned into Cadmus. It was apparent that whatever was coming next was evil. Lonely howls came first, blood-curling and loud, before a massive wall of black, ragged fur stepped into view.

Cerberus. I knew it before I even saw it. The three-headed demon dog that guarded the gates of hell. The smell of sulfur and rotted flesh filled the air around us and I fought an overwhelming urge to cover my nose with my hand.

One of the three heads turned slowly and met my gaze. I tried not to blink, to not be the first to look away, but it was difficult. There was ugliness in its eyes. Cold and flat, I knew those eyes had seen evil that I couldn't even imagine. Every horrendous thing that had ever crossed the gates of hell had passed this guardian first. Its large wild eye rolled and then the head swiveled to look again at the crowd. I felt a sense of relief that I was no longer in its line of vision. The beast was unnerving.

Cadmus caught my eye, his eyebrow raised as if to ask if I was okay. I nodded, squeezing his hand. He pulled me closer and then wrapped his arm around my shoulders. His warmth was reassuring and I melted into it as we watched the parade of evil pour from the underworld.

More and more beasts emerged from the open gateway. With each one, the air around us grew colder and colder. The evil in the air was palpable. I only hoped that the chieftains and Hecate could control these creatures as well as they thought they could.

Finally, as far as my eyes could see, there was an ocean of armed warriors, beasts from hell and gods and goddesses from my homeland. United with a common cause, everyone stood together. It was humbling and breathtaking at once. Good and evil would battle together to face an adversary that was the most evil of all.

"We should hear from the Chosen One!" someone screamed and I startled. I had never been one for the limelight. I always traveled safely behind the scenes, guiding those around me. I had never grown accustomed to walking in the spotlight.

I swallowed hard.

"They wish to hear from you, love," Cadmus prompted. "Do you feel up to it?" He searched my face quickly, his chocolate eyes concerned. "You do not have to."

"Of course I do," I replied. "They are willing to die today. The least I can do is speak to them."

He grinned, a beautiful smile of reassurance and encouragement and I drew comfort from it. In it, I found a reminder that this was a man that loved me so much that he would protect me with his life. I brushed a soft kiss on his cheek as I passed him, walking to the front. As I stepped forward, the crowd cheered.

"I am Harmonia," I called. At my voice, everyone stilled. It became so quiet that I could hear the breaths from the horses. "I am the goddess of peace and contentment. And I have been told that I am the Chosen One, that I am meant to bring peace to us all." There were nods and shouts and I paused to scan the crowd.

"I must tell you that I do not feel like a Chosen One," I continued.

Murmurings. Restlessness. Soft gasps.

I raised my arm and held my birthmark in the air for all to see.

"I have been marked for so long that I do not remember a time when I was not. I was misled to believe that I was something that I was not and have inadvertently done heinous things. All because of the whims of three ancient women. Their desire for power and recognition has tumbled a great city, Olympus, to rubble. The powerful gods and goddesses within have been taken. The machinations of these women have turned the mortal world into something ugly and evil…something that it is not. We are the only ones left to set everything right and restore everything to that which it should be.

"I might not feel like the Chosen One, but apparently that is exactly what I am. I died earlier today. Then I returned to this life, gasping for air like a fish on the edge of a pond, my wounds miraculously healed. For whatever reason, I am meant to be here right now and *you* were meant to be here right now. I am grateful to you for riding with me this day. Together, we will change the world and we will emerge victorious."

Utter silence.

Then everyone erupted into shouts and yells. Horses reared and stomped, people called my name. Never, for the rest of my immortal life, would I forget the feelings from this day. Hope, fear, pride and trepidation swirled together in my chest and the emotions threatened to overwhelm me as my eyes welled up with tears.

Cadmus grabbed me from behind and clasped me to him, circled by his strong arms.

"You are the most beautiful, amazing creature ever to walk the earth," he told me softly. "I have never been so proud to be your husband and there is no place I would rather be than with you. I have been a warrior for centuries. But today, I feel at home with you by my side. We will fight together, my love, and we will win together. And then we will return together for our daughter."

I nodded as he kissed my lips, his mouth soft and gentle. I felt a tear streak down my cheek and he wiped it away.

"Do not cry," he whispered, leaning his forehead against mine. "We will be victorious and all will be well." I nodded, sniffling as he took a finger and wiped my tears.

"I love you, wife."

"And I love you," I replied.

Turning, we once again faced our army as we prepared to ride into battle.

CHAPTER TWENTY-ONE

The palace grounds were quiet and dark as we approached, our horses' hooves clacking against the packed dirt road beneath us. Above us, Ortrera and her Amazon warriors circled, their muscled legs guiding their Pegasus' while they kept their eyes trained on the ground below them. I glanced up and Ortrera shook her head. Apparently, she saw nothing.

Not a sound, not a movement came from within the compound. The silence was deafening. Even though it was only late afternoon, the dark clouds that swirled around us gave the appearance of the dead of night. The darkened palace loomed in front of us, ominous and stark behind the stone walls.

Ares rode in front, with my mother, Cadmus, Hecate and me at his flanks. The legions of undead warriors fell in behind us, while gods and goddesses from the Spiritlands brought up the tail. The beasts from hell were situated throughout. They carried with them their acidic, sulfurous smell.

"Where is everyone?" I murmured to Cadmus. "This place seems deserted."

"Trust me, it is not," he replied, looking around cautiously. "They only want to appear that way. It's a brilliant tactic."

If by brilliant, he meant unsettling, then I agreed. The hair rose on the hackles of my neck as I glanced around us.

Shadows drifted around every corner as we moved stealthily toward the compound, the eerie silence roaring in my ears.

And then all hell broke loose.

Alarms sounded, the bugles screeching into the countryside and Arthur's men were suddenly everywhere. Our horses' hindquarters ground into the dirt to find traction as we pivoted and spun, trying to keep our backs safe from attack.

"Stay with me!"Cadmus shouted to me, brandishing a gleaming sword as he whirled in his saddle. The broadside of his weapon came into contact with Sir Gareth's young chest. Gareth's face, which was normally so boyish and handsome, was twisted into an ugly sneer as he tumbled from his horse and then leaped back to his feet.

"Worry about yourself!" I called, as I spun Celine in a circle.

Hefting a lance from the rings attached to my saddle, I used goddess strength to hurl it toward Sir Gareth. Flying with such velocity, it easily sliced through the armor protecting his arm and embedded into the earth. The tip buried at least three feet into the ground, effectively pinning the angry knight. He was uninjured, but there was no way he would be getting up any time soon.

"Well done," Cadmus grinned.

"Let us try not to injure them," I suggested. "They are not themselves."

"Agreed," Cadmus replied. "They have been my brothers for a long while. I do not wish to harm them."

Ahead of me, I watched my mother pin a young knight and his squire to the wall of the castle with her silvery goddess gaze. Another squire, attempting to grab her from behind was thwarted by my father.

With a deafening roar, Ares grabbed the teenaged boy, squeezing him tightly around the ribs. I heard a loud crack before he tossed the boy limply aside. The boy didn't move. He wasn't dead, but broken ribs would keep him immobile and would prevent him from rejoining the battle. It seemed that we were all of the same mind--- to avoid killing these soldiers.

In front of me, Cerebrus sat calmly, while Bedivere and Lamarak charged toward him. Their faces glistened with hate, their armor clattered as they launched themselves at him. Cerebrus reared his head back and breathed a mouthful of horrendous gas toward the knights.

It knocked them over and Bedivere retched into the dirt.

"By God, that is vile!" he shouted. "It smells like death."

"He eats death for dinner, my brother," Cadmus replied from behind them.

With that, he drew a short sword, approaching the two knights in the dirt. Both of them lunged to their feet, drawing their weapons to fight. While they parried to and fro, the Cerebrus watched with glistening black eyes, its mane of snakes writhing along its great neck. It caused me to shudder before I turned my attention back to the battle raging around me.

Just as I was deciding where to intercede, the sky around me turned a deep, bloody red. Gasping in surprise, I turned my face to the sun and found that it had turned black. Gray, thunderous clouds rolled through the crimson sky and a hideous wailing filled the land.

I covered my ears with my hands, unable to stand the horrifying shrieks.

"What is it?" I screamed to Aphrodite. She whirled in a circle and then lunged to the top of the palace wall, crouching as she searched the horizon. But then I saw them myself and my blood turned to ice.

The Fates were descending from the sky, each of them coming upon us as demons. They flew with massive black wings, the skin stretched taut over pointy bone. Their naked bodies were covered in black scales, their eyes as black as pitch. They possessed tails and fangs and claws and they were without a doubt the most terrifying creatures I had ever seen. They were evil personified.

My mother leapt from the wall to stand with me and we circled, keeping our backs together in order to protect ourselves. As the Fates landed on the ground, they walked on all fours, their curled claws scraping the earth loudly as they moved.

I gulped.

"This isn't good, mother," I observed.

"Whatever gave you that idea?" she asked lightly. "They are nothing, daughter. Do not be intimidated."

I looked around and found that the knights did not appear surprised at anything on this battlefield... not the hounds from hell, not the bronzed fire-breathing horses, not the Fates themselves. The mortal world had certainly changed. They were simply accustomed now to expecting the worst at all times. I shook my head at the misery of that existence.

Lachesis caught my eye and stepped from the middle of her sisters, her black eyes snapping and gleaming as she approached. I swallowed hard and gripped my dagger tightly.

"What will you do with that, keeper?" she hissed as she drew up in front of me to her full height. In this new demon form, she was seven feet tall. Her fangs glistened in the eerie red light and I felt chills run down the length of my legs.

"Perhaps I will drive it into your black heart," I suggested as I turned it over and over in my hands.

My mother stood rigidly against my back, protecting me from any unexpected attack as I faced the middle Moirae sister. Ares was engaged with the other two, his muscles straining as they fought. I blocked it out. My thoughts had to focus on this one sister. This was my fight.

"Why you?" I asked her seriously. "Why has it always been you that tormented me? It has always been you that visited me in so many lives, it has been you that thought of ways to torture me. I am betting it was you who chose to take my child from me and hide her away with Calypso. Why?"

She threw her frightening head back and laughed, but her laugh now sounded like a hissing shriek. My heart stilled at the sound, but I showed no outward sign of fear.

"Of course it was me!" she exclaimed proudly. "It has always been me that understood what a threat you would eventually become. My sisters didn't believe it," she sneered. "Even though the prophecy was clear, they couldn't fathom that the weak girl that we had thrust into mortal form so many times could actually challenge us."

She appraised me, her onyx gaze glittering. "But I knew."

"I'm not weak," I replied. "I've never been weak."

"No," she answered thoughtfully, her voice frighteningly calm. "You haven't. But you are weaker than me. I dine on little goddesses like you."

Anger surged within me, fury at everything she had done to me over the millennia combining to fuel my rage.

"Try it," I snarled, leaping toward her. "I dare you."

She lunged and met me mid-air, her wings closing in to clasp me to her within the diaphanous folds. Her skin was slippery and sticky at once and I struggled against her. Her fetid breath was moist on my neck, the tip of one fang scratching my skin.

"I'm going to drink every drop of your blood," she breathed into my ear. "And then I will have your daughter's for an evening cocktail."

She shouldn't have threatened Raquel.

My rage filled my fingertips and exploded, throwing Lachesis off of me. She flew into the palace wall and rolled to the ground, but quickly leaped back to her feet. Out of my periphery, I found that Cadmus had joined Ares now and they were engaged with the other two Moirae sisters.

"Harmonia, are you alright?" Cadmus called, not taking his eyes from Atropos. He held Zeus' sword in his hand, raising it parallel with her face. She hissed at him in response, lifting one clawed hand to scratch at the ground in front of her.

"I'm fine," I answered, keeping my gaze locked with Lachesis. She grinned, a horrifying, grotesque sight.

"Are you?" she asked. "I don't think you are."

She advanced on me once again, taking slow steps. I didn't move back, choosing instead to stand my ground. This was going to end here, today. There was no point in retreating.

To my right, Hecate screamed as Kay thrust his sword deep into her shoulder. I gasped as blood gushed from the wound. He stared into her face as she slid from his sword to the ground.

"What think you now, witch?" he snarled and I gasped again. Kay had always been my favorite because of his kind spirit. There was no trace of kindness in him now. Any gentleness in his spirit had been sucked away by this strange new world.

Around me, screams and vicious shouts prevailed and as I watched the vicious fighting, I realized that neither side would prevail here. Arthur's soldiers would fight to the death, the Fates would ensure that.

"Hecate, can you stand?" I called.

"Of course," she muttered, climbing slowly to her feet. Kay's sword could not kill her, but the wound was clearly painful. Blood drenched the entire left side of her body and her face was ghostly pale.

"You need to retreat to the Spiritlands," I called, trying to circle nearer to her, as my mother intercepted to distract Kay. Lachesis followed me, stepping around the fallen soldiers with no regard to their moans.

"Take the sword with you," I continued, finally reaching her side. "And keep watch. At my signal, plunge it into the sheath next to Zeus' throne. I think that's the only way. It's the only way we'll fix all of these atrocities. But first, we must defeat the Fates."

"Good luck with that, Keeper," Lachesis hissed. Ignoring her, I called to my husband.

"Lucan?"

From a few yards away, Cadmus lifted his head and his chocolaty gaze met mine. He had blood smeared on his cheek.

"Lucan, Hecate needs the sword."

He nodded curtly and began to fight his way toward us, holding Percivale and Gareth at bay while he moved. His skill was unmistakable and I couldn't help but admire it, even in the midst of our current danger. I had seen him fight many times, but never while I was at his side. It was a heady thing to behold.

It took him a scant few moments to reach us before he pressed the sword into Hecate's hand, wrapping her bloody fingers around it. She staggered, leaned into Cadmus and then righted herself.

"Hecate!" I cried.

"I'm fine," she reassured me weakly. "I'll wait for your signal."

And she was gone.

The knights nearest to us looked around nervously.

"Where did the witch go?" Kay wondered, looking first over his shoulder and then at the horizon.

"Away from you," I replied harshly, staring him in the eye. He didn't flinch. "I'm sorry that this has happened to you, Kay. You were once a good man."

"Goodness is overrated," he sneered before lunging toward me once more, his once handsome face turned ugly by hate. Cadmus stopped him with a knife to the heart. Kay staggered a few steps and then fell.

"Lucan!" I cried. "Do not kill them!"

He barely glanced at me as he returned to battle once more. "Woman, if it is him or you, my choice will always be you."

He strode back into the fray without a backward glance, intent on covering Ares' vulnerable flank. Panic began to set in. I somehow innately knew that in order to emerge as victors, we had to defeat the Fates first before restoring the sword. The problem was... how?

I looked around and found fighting everywhere, as far as my eyes could see. Knights that we were once noble and valiant were now fighting with no honor or code. And what was even worse, as I felt myself being watched, I slowly turned to find Arthur seated atop a knoll beyond the edge of the fighting. He was safely out of harm's way, watching his knights fight for him. The old Arthur would never do that. He fought on the front lines, leading his soldiers to battle.

He sat with his royal blue cloak fluttering around him, perfectly outlined by the red sky. His icy blue eyes impaling me from across the field with his stare. He was much different from the last time I had seen him. Malice had lined his handsome face and I found I had to look away. I just couldn't bear to see him in such a way.

My mother's shrieks of rage drew my attention once more and I raced to her side to help fend off Lachesis. Lachesis had straightened to her full height and was hovering over my mother. Suddenly, they locked arms, my mother's goddess strength pitted evenly against the evil that fueled Lachesis. My mother's arms shook with the effort and her silver eyes met mine.

"Now, Harmonia!"

I remembered the dagger in my hand and closing the distance between us in two bounds, I thrust it into Lachesis' black heart, burying it to the hilt. Her eyes widened and her breath exhaled in a hiss. Her arms dropped from my mother and she hit the ground hard on her knees. The ground shook from her weight and she toppled, face first into the dirt.

I rushed to my mother, embracing her.

"We did it!" I cried in astonishment. "We did it."

But Aphrodite was looking past me over my shoulder, shaking her head in shock.

"No, we didn't," she replied. I turned and found Lachesis once again lumbering to her feet, my dagger still embedded in her heart. She looked at me and laughed.

"Did you really think it would be so easy?"

In one fluid motion, she leaped to where I stood, knocking my mother out of the way. Lifting me by my neck, she held me high in the air as I gasped to breathe.

"You will die," she said calmly, ice dripping from her words. "Somehow."

I couldn't breathe. Lack of oxygen was blurring my vision and as I gasped, everything around me seemed to turn into slow-motion. Cadmus had his back to me, helping my father fight Clothos. My mother was crumpled motionlessly on the ground to my left and Ortrera was struggling against a group of five knights to my right. Screams and howls filled the air and the smell of blood filled my nose as I allowed my eyes to flutter closed. Perhaps she would win after all. I didn't even have the breath left to scream.

But I didn't have to. Another horrible screech filled the air and I opened my eyes weakly. Merlin was seated atop a massive beast on the horizon. From here, it seemed to be as large as an elephant and most definitely was the most terrifying sight I had ever beheld.

The creature had the body of a massive bull, but the fangs of a lion. His giant horns extended for two feet on each side before curling around. Each horn was as thick as my thigh, his giant hooves cloven. His eyes were blood red, his lips thick and curled back, exposing his massive fangs. Even on the verge of passing out as I was, the sight of him made my heart race.

Behind them, the three ancient Keres floated in mid-air. They were horrifying and each looked like a rotting corpse. Their faces were pale and wrinkled, their eyes streaming blood. But their gazes were all fixated on me.

"Now!" Merlin bellowed and his voice filled the countryside. The Keres launched into flight, their voluminous cloaks streaming behind them as they aimed for me.

CHAPTER TWENTY-TWO

As the three ancient hags separated in the air, Thanatos aimed for Clothos, Ker hurtled toward Atropos and Moros threw herself into Lachesis, knocking me from the Moirae's grasp. I tumbled to the ground and lay gasping as I tried to fill my lungs with much-needed oxygen.

Cadmus shoved through the masses of people around him to get to my side, kneeling next to me.

"My love," he said anxiously. "Are you alright?"

I nodded, keeping my eyes on the mid-air battle above me. All three Keres were warring with the three Moirae in an epic battle that the world had never seen before. Their shrill shrieks split the sky as claws flew and blood dripped to the ground below.

"By the gods," he breathed in disbelief.

The Keres fought with everything they had, and the Moirae returned each effort back to them. It was a grotesquely fascinating sight. Scrambling to my hands and knees, I crawled to my mother, turning her over.

"Mother," I murmured, shaking her. "Mother, open your eyes." Her eyes opened and I stared into the silvery depths. "You have to see this."

Obligingly, she lifted her gaze to the sky and then her eyes widened. None of us had ever seen such a thing. We silently sat watching as the scene in front of us unfolded.

Lachesis lunged, her fangs taking a chunk from Moros' shoulder. Moros screeched and charged back, her claws ripping at Lachesis' throat. Blood flowed but none of them fell. But then, Moros ducked her head, her cloudy stare directed intensely at me.

"Open the gates!" she ordered. "Open them now."

Open the gates? I was bewildered for a moment before realization washed over me in a cold wave. She was talking about the gates of hell. I quickly appealed to Hecate, muttering my request.

"Hecate, please open the gates. Open the gates," I murmured. When nothing happened, I screamed. "Open the gates!" My voice was shrill and carried far across the Camelot hills and I knew that if Hecate was watching, she would hear.

And the ground opened up.

The horrifying screams from hell floated from the underworld and Moros smiled a deathly, bloody grin.

"It is done, Keeper."

With that, she and her sisters used their remaining strength to drag the Moirae with them into the yawning, black tunnel. The Moirae's screams were futile, because they weren't strong enough to stop it. I saw the tips of someone's black cloak swirling into the hole before the other hounds of hell followed them. Then the hole closed up, the grass where it had been completely undisturbed.

Everything was still, as everyone around us remained frozen in the sudden silence.

"It is done," I repeated, wrinkling my forehead. I looked to Cadmus. "It is done?"

He nodded. "It must be."

Before anyone could move or resume their fight, I shouted at Hecate. I knew for sure she was watching us now.

"It is done, witch. *Do it now!*" I cried.

I envisioned her plunging the sword of Zeus into the onyx scabbard next to his throne, freeing the world of the Fates' rule. I imagined that any minute, we would witness an explosion or earthquakes or something of equal magnitude.

For a moment nothing happened. Everything remained the same and the small skirmishes began to continue around me. Just when I was looking to Cadmus in confusion, the earth rumbled and I froze.

The sky's brilliant red hue faded to cloudy white then to blue. The sun broke free from clouds and began to shine brightly and I lifted my face to its warmth. The undead chieftains were gone and I happily assumed that they were now at rest.

"It is happening," I cried joyfully to Cadmus. "We did it!"

Under our feet, as we watched, the brown dead grasses turned green, fluttering lightly as the cool, refreshing breeze blew. Rain began to fall and as it soaked my hair and clothing, I had never been happier in my life.

"We did it!" I cried again, wrapping my wet arms around Cadmus' neck and pulling him down for a celebratory kiss. "We did it."

Over Cadmus' shoulder, I spotted Arthur, still perched on the hill top. His face was confused for a moment, then it regained his customary kind expression. I began to raise my hand to wave to him, when I noticed his gaze harden on Ares.

"What..." my voice trailed off as I watched Arthur gesture his knights into formation. They each picked themselves from the ground, even Kay who had been killed, and formed themselves behind their king, ready for battle.

"What is going on?" I asked in bewilderment. The knights were no longer the hardened killers that they had been a moment ago, but they clearly were riding toward Ares now.

And then it occurred to me.

"Oh, dear god no."

Time had been restored, which meant that Arthur was being forced into fighting Lancelot for sleeping with Guinevere. Mordred, who was even now riding directly behind the king in the champion's normal position, had arranged for Arthur to find Guinevere and Lancelot together. Arthur had no choice but to act. Lancelot and Guinevere had committed treason and Arthur was nothing if not fair.

"Father!" I cried. Ares turned his large head toward me, his eyes filled with sadness.

"I know, Harmonia," he replied tiredly.

He knew that Mordred's actions would be the death of Arthur this day and there wasn't anything we do to stop it. In resignation, he turned to face the advancing knights, all of them his brothers-in-arms.

Just when I thought we had won, it appeared that once more, all would be lost in Camelot. But this time, it was simply history repeating itself. Sadness welled in my heart as I observed the scene around me.

My mother, tattered and beautiful, lay curled on the green grasses. Ares, powerful and brave, stood ready to fight a legion of his brothers. My husband, skilled and strong, stood at my father's side. I climbed to my feet and crossed to my mother's side, picking up her limp hand.

"Lancelot," Arthur called. "You were my most trusted knight. I valued you above all others in my army. You were as a brother. But you repaid me by dishonoring my wife. What have you to say?"

My father leveled his dark gaze at the king that he so respected. There was truly nothing to say, for Arthur was right. While here in Camelot, my mother was Arthur's wife. Both she and Lancelot had disrespected her vows and the king.

Ares lowered his sword and dropped his head.

"I beg your forgiveness, your highness," he said. "You are correct. I have wronged you in a most grievous way."

"But it was not his fault!" a clear voice rang out.

Turning in surprise, I found Morgan, her skirts fluttering in the wind around her legs, facing the king behind us.

"It was I," she continued, "Who bewitched your trusted knight and your wife. It is I who has done this wretched thing to you, my brother."

A collective gasp rippled through the crowd and I found myself overwhelmed by confusion. What was Eris doing?

"Can this be true?" Arthur asked and I could see on his face that he would give anything to make it so. Morgan nodded without hesitation.

"It is true, brother. I beg your forgiveness and will do anything to repay you for my transgressions. I have been horrendous to you of late, as you know. I beg you to forgive me. But even if you cannot, please do not hold Lancelot and the queen accountable. They could not help their actions. My magic is powerful."

Arthur stared at her sharply, his thoughts evident on his face. He believed her and he lowered his lance.

As he did, Mordred spoke from behind.

"Your highness, your sister has admitted to using witchery. How can we trust her? She is most likely lying to you."

The king didn't turn, but spoke with his gaze frozen lovingly on my mother.

"Do you think I do not know my sister, good knight? I know her character and her heart. She speaks the truth."

Arthur slid from his horse and strode toward my mother, his face flooded with love. He paused for just a moment where Ares knelt, placing his hand silently on his knight's shoulder. Then he continued, quickly crossing the field.

"Guinevere, I am sorry that I doubted you," he called as he approached. "I will never doubt you again."

"Because you are a fool!" Mordred snarled from behind him, leaping from his horse and lunging toward Arthur with his sword drawn.

Arthur whirled, surprise freezing his handsome features and he barely had time to draw his own sword in order to defend himself. His knights quickly approached, flying to their king's aid, but I froze as I saw the horizon.

Lines and lines of mounted Saxons were poised and ready to ride toward us.

"What the..." I breathed. My mother gripped my hand tightly as we watched the riders approach.

"Saxons," my mother said quietly. "Mordred must have bought them to topple Arthur. Mordred knew he could never turn the Roundtable knights, so he went outside of the kingdom."

A split moment later, Mordred confirmed her theory.

"Gunner," Mordred called to one of them with a menacing smile. "You are very timely. Kill them all!"

The Saxon mercenary grinned in response, a menacing gesture that stilled my heart. He would have been handsome, with sandy blonde hair and hazel eyes, but his cold calculation only made him deadly instead. He pushed into the knights swinging two swords at once.

Once again, mortal combat broke out around us. My mother and I stared at each other helplessly as we moved to the perimeter of the field. We weren't sure what to do. This battle was meant to take place and we had already seen what changing time could do.

We stood still, watching the bloody men fighting in front of us. I watched Cadmus fighting a Saxon and took a step toward him.

"No," my mother cautioned. "You know you cannot."

I froze in place, my heart numb as I watched the Saxon swing a mace into Cadmus' leg. I cried out and gripped my mother's arm tightly.

"I cannot stand here and do nothing!" I cried. "This is impossible."

Cadmus crumbled to the ground, but as the Saxon swung his sword for a death blow, Cadmus blocked it with his own.

"Lucan won't die by that Saxon's hand," my mother said knowingly. And he didn't. He fought the Saxon off and plunged his sword into his opponent's heart before he staggered into Bedivere. Bedivere wrapped his arm around Cadmus' shoulders and helped him walk as they limped toward Arthur and Mordred.

Arthur and Mordred were fighting hand to hand. Arthur had shed his cloaks and he stood facing his nephew in a shirt and trousers. He already had a thin line of blood on his shoulder where Mordred had sliced him.

"Heleyne," Arthur called. "Is my wife alright?"

I startled. I couldn't believe that he would take his focus from his adversary to ask such a question.

"She is fine, your highness," I answered limply.

"Too bad we cannot say the same for you," Mordred sneered and he plunged his sword once more into Arthur's shoulder, bringing his uncle to his knees with a shout.

Arthur wrenched away in time for Kay to intercept Mordred's next blow, returning it with equal force and sliding his sword smoothly under Mordred's ribcage.

"Ah, Kay the dependable," Arthur said gratefully. "Thank you, my brother."

Kay nodded, switching his sword from hand to hand as he faced Mordred.

"If you want another swipe at my brother," he growled. "You will have to come through me."

"Gladly," Mordred sneered and he motioned his army of Saxons forward.

Gunner, the lead mercenary, charged forward and plunged his sword into Kay's thigh. With a groan, Kay dropped to the ground and I heard a loud crunching noise as the large Saxon withdrew his sword. I cringed. That noise was Kay's split thigh bone.

Every knight was preoccupied defending their lives against the Saxons and there was not one left who was available to protect Kay in his injured state.

Gunner planted a thick boot into Kay's chest , knocking him over and as Kay lay heaving for breath, Gunner brought his foot forcefully down into Kay's skull. I heard a loud crack and Kay lay limply, his eyes sightlessly staring straight ahead.

A tear slipped down my cheek. There wasn't a thing I could do about these atrocities. These were man-made and I couldn't interfere, but they were ripping my heart from my chest.

With Kay out of the way, Mordred advanced once more on Arthur. As Arthur lunged forward, Mordred tripped him and Arthur stumbled. Using the momentum, Mordred plunged his thick sword into Arthur's back. Arthur cried out, a horrible cry of agony, before whirling and embedding his own sword into Mordred's side. Blood gushed and Mordred twisted away, crawling toward the hilltop.

Arthur dropped to the ground, his breathing shallow and quick.

"Guinevere," he called weakly.

My mother opened her eyes. She was wounded, but even in her weakened state, she could hear the life fading from his voice. She staggered to her feet and leaning into me, we limped to where Arthur lay in a pool of blood. She dropped to his side, picking up his hand.

"I'm so sorry, Arthur," she murmured, stroking his hair back from his face. "You did not deserve this."

"I did not?" he asked simply. "I did not deserve a beautiful wife and the love of an entire country? I have been blessed, wife. Do not cry for me," he said as he watched tears stream down her cheeks. "I will leave here at peace, for I have done what I was sent here to do."

His eyes fluttered closed and my chest froze. I couldn't breathe or swallow the lump in my throat at the sight of this great fallen king. My mother continued to hold his hand as every knight in the field dropped to one knee and lowered his head in deference to Arthur. Even the Saxons stood still, allowing the Britons a moment to honor their dead king.

Except for one. Gunner stealthily crept behind Cadmus and Bedivere, his cold hazel eyes focused with unwavering clarity on his target. His face was as menacing as I'd ever seen.

"Lucan!" I screamed, gesturing wildly toward Gunner.

But it was too late. Cadmus barely had time to turn, injured as he already was, before Gunner's lance ran him through. Cadmus' head was thrown back and he hung limply on the lance, his feet shaking, before Gunner yanked it away. Cadmus dropped to the ground.

I cried out, then watched gratefully as Bedivere drew his sword and charged at Gunner, strategically drawing the Saxon away from my husband. Cadmus lay flat on his back, his chest shuddering slowly as blood poured from his gaping wound. I knew I wouldn't get there in time if I ran like a mortal, so I materialized next to his side in the blink of an eye. I didn't care who saw me.

Cadmus' eyes were already turning cloudy and I collapsed onto his chest.

"I cannot do this again, Cadmus," I cried. "This is too horrible, too wrong. Please, my love. Please."

He stared at me weakly, raising one shaking hand to my face, resting his fingers against my lips.

"Harmonia, you know this isn't forever. I shall see you in a moment. I will wake in the Spiritlands, I promise you. Come meet me there."

"You promise you'll be there?" I uttered haltingly.
Blood dripped from my husband's lips and he couldn't speak but he nodded. That was the last movement he would make. His chest shuddered to a stop and he died. My screams were loud enough to reach the corners of the earth.

CHAPTER TWENTY-THREE

A moment later, I felt my mother's cool hands on my shoulders.

"Harmonia, do not weep. We are done here. It is done. Let us return home, where I know Cadmus is waiting."

I turned into her embrace, unable to stop the flow of my tears. Over her shoulder, I saw Lucan's lifeless body crumpled into the grass and I squeezed my eyes tightly closed. This never got any easier.

Ares and Ahmose joined us and my mother called to Hecate.

The next thing I knew, we were standing in the flowering courtyard of Zeus' palace.

As soon as I opened my eyes and realized where I was, I took off like lightning through the falling lotus blossoms for the palace doors. Flying inside, I streaked up the marble steps to my bedchambers. Throwing open the doors, I pushed past Ortrera's warriors and stopped short.

Cadmus was sitting on the table where I had left him. As he looked up and saw me, his face lit up in a grin and he stood, opening his strong arms. I flew into him with a crash and we toppled over onto the cushions.

"I can never watch you die again," I cried as tears streaked down my cheeks and fell onto him. "I cannot do it. Are you listening?"

He laughed, the most welcome sound I had ever heard, as he stroked my hair.

"I'm here now, my love. There is no need for tears."

"As if I can help it," I sniffed.

"Have I mentioned lately that you're very beautiful?" he asked with a smile. "There has never been a woman in all of history who has been as lovely as you are."

"Don't change the subject," I growled against his neck as I showered him in kisses. "I am never, ever, *ever* going to watch you die again. I can't believe you put me through it."

"As if I had a choice," he replied wryly. "The wastelands were no picnic, I can assure you."

I inhaled him, stroking his face and his chest before kissing him soundly. I didn't want to take my hands from him—I wanted to stay with him forever. After seeing how lifeless he was in the Wastelands, I would never get enough of his vitality. I would absorb it if I could.

"That was horrible, I agree," I said softly. "But you're here now. And trust me, I'm never letting you go again."

I climbed off of him and pulled him to his feet. "Let us go and get Raquel," I urged. "Let us get our daughter."

He studied me for a brief moment before smiling. "Perhaps, just maybe, you might want to change your clothing first."

I glanced down and found my dress tattered and blood-stained. My hair was a tangled mess. I looked like I had just fought a battle, which of course, I had.

"You might be right," I agreed. Waving my hand, I dressed myself in a clean white frock and my hair was instantly arranged in a neat chignon.

"Better?" I grinned.

"Almost," he replied, wiping at a smear of blood on my chin. "Now you're perfect."

Leaning up, I kissed him softly on the mouth, leaning into him as he deepened the kiss. He tasted like sunshine and I vowed never to move from his arms.

Someone cleared their throat from the doorway and I turned my head to find Aphrodite watching us with a smirk.

"I told you so, Harmonia," she announced. "I knew Cadmus would be here and all would be well."

My thoughts returned to the knights of the roundtable, slain on that bloody field.

"Some of us are well," I answered softly. "Only some of us."

She studied me for a moment, her lovely face thoughtful.

"Harmonia, we cannot change the mortal world. They eventually die. And those knights, they died with valor, the way they all prayed to go."

"Your mother is right," Ares announced from behind Aphrodite. He walked past her to scoop me up in a hearty bear hug and squeezed me until I couldn't breathe.

"Knights prefer to die in glory," he confirmed. "They all died a good soldier's death."

I nodded. I knew he was right. Every knight, every warrior of any type for that matter, wanted to die in battle.

Harmonia.

Ahmose' voice resounded in my head.

I'm proud of you.

His voice drew me to the window and I stared down, finding Ahmose in the courtyard looking back up at me. He was alive and well and back to his true self, an ancient man with black robes and thick eye-makeup. His black eyes glittered in the sun as brilliant blue lotus blossoms fell from the tree above him, fluttering around his feet.

I'm proud of you. But it isn't over.

I rolled my eyes and shook my head. Could he not let me enjoy it for just a moment? Of course it wasn't over. We still had to find where the Fates had imprisoned the Olympian gods and that would most likely be no small feat. But for now, the imminent threats were behind us and that called for a small celebration.

Right after I retrieved my daughter.

I grabbed Cadmus' hand and pulled him past my parents and out of the room, calling over my shoulder.

"You should plan a dinner, mother. This is cause for celebration!"

"Did she just say that she wanted a party?" I heard my mother ask in surprise. I had to smile. She was right. I was normally not one for parties. But we were bringing our daughter home and that was cause for a party if ever there was one.

"We've got to get back to Thalassa," I told Cadmus as I pulled him along behind me. "She has Raquel."

"Calm yourself, wife," he instructed patiently. "She'll still be there when we arrive. There is no need to break our necks in the process."

At his words, he neatly caught a large vase that I knocked over with my shoulder as I flew past. I laughed and slowed down. He was right. We had been separated from her for several millennia. A few minutes more would not kill us.

As I forced myself to walk slowly down the stairs, I could feel Cadmus containing his laughter behind me, but chose to ignore it. Any mother in her right mind would feel excited in my position and I wasn't going to try and contain it.

"We should find Hecate before we travel to Avalon Lake," I murmured to him excitedly.

"Did you call for me?"

Hecate appeared behind Cadmus, a brilliant white smile on her lovely face. I shook my head. It has always been said that mortals enjoyed instant gratification. Mortals had nothing on gods.

"Hecate, we must get to Thalassa. I must see my daughter before I explode," I rushed and she laughed, but her face grew serious.

"Harmonia, I have to caution you…something isn't right. I can feel it."

"What in the world do you mean, Hecate?" I stared at her in confusion.

"Zeus' sword…" she began haltingly. "No one can control it like he can and I'm afraid… I'm afraid all did not go as planned."

My heart stuttered.

"What do you mean?" I whispered.

"I sheathed Zeus' sword as planned. And as I did, I offered incantations to undo the Fates' influence. But I feel as though that was not the correct thing to do."

"What do you mean, witch? Of course it was the correct thing to do. The Fates manipulated so many things throughout the millennia. Of course it needed to stop."

She nodded. "Going forward, yes," she agreed. "But I fear that my incantations have changed some things that we would not have wished to change. And my spell was permanent. It will take Zeus to set it right now."

"What things have been changed?" I asked hesitantly.

"Raquel…" Hecate's voice trailed off.

The breath froze on my lips as Cadmus' grip tightened in alarm on my arm.

"My daughter?" I whispered.

Without waiting to say another word or ask another question, I faded from the Spiritlands and reappeared on the banks next to Avalon Lake. The mists hung heavy over the water, the lush grasses thick with dew.

"Thalassa?" I called, scanning the area. No one was here but me. "Thalassa?" I called again.

Hecate and Cadmus appeared a few yards away, my husband's face frantic until he caught sight of me. He rushed to my side.

"Did you find her?" he asked anxiously. I shook my head.

As I did, I noticed ripples forming from the center of the lake. Watching with frozen breath, I waited while Thalassa emerged, walking out of her home beneath the lake. Dripping, she approached me with a smile, holding out her hand.

"Harmonia!" she called joyfully. "I'm so happy that you were victorious!"

She clasped my hand with her cold wet one and grinned again. "Well done!"

"Thalassa," I began quickly. "Where is Raquel?"

She stared at me blankly. "Raquel?" she repeated.

"My daughter," I replied impatiently. "Where is she? You were protecting her. Where is she?" My voice turned shrill and my heart dropped in my chest at the continued look of confusion on Thalassa's ethereal face.

"I don't know what you mean," she said uncertainly, shifting her weight as she stared at me. "I don't know her."

Hecate broke in gently. "This is what I was trying to tell you. I'm afraid that anything that the Fates had a direct hand in, such as the birth of your daughter, has been skewed or undone. It might be as though your daughter never existed. Or if she does, I do not know where."

My gaze flew to my husband's face. He was as horrified as I was.

"How do we find her?" he asked, automatically pulling me to his chest. I dropped my forehead against him as I waited for the answer and when it came, I found that I already knew it.

"We must find Zeus," Hecate answered firmly. "He is the only one who can truly command his sword. And with his sword, all can be restored."

They kept talking but their voices faded from my consciousness. I limply rested against Cadmus, shock overwhelming me until it felt I would collapse. With my eyes closed, I felt his strong arms scoop me up and hold me firmly against him.

When I opened my eyes again, I was in my bed in the Spiritlands with my mother fluttering around me like a bird. She was packing my knapsack as Cadmus sat on the edge of the bed, stroking my hand gently.

"Are you alright?" he asked in concern. My eyes welled up with tears and I couldn't answer.

"My love," he began. "All will be well. Look at how far we've come. The Fates are trapped in the underworld and they will never escape, Cerberus will see to that. Without their intervention, we will find Zeus before you know it. And with Zeus' power, all will be restored, just as Hecate said."

"Do you really believe that?" I whispered, keeping my gaze fixed on his handsome face.

"Of course I do," he replied firmly. "We're together now and we shall never be separated again. We have this one final quest, this one last journey to complete, before everything is made perfect and whole again. We will find our daughter and our family will be complete."

He sounded so certain, so sure, that I could scarcely doubt it. And I knew that he was right. We had come so far, traveling over oceans of time already. What was one last journey? We had the powers of the Spiritlands and my bloodstone at our fingertips and we would search every corner of the earth. It was not impossible.

I nodded limply, grasping his hand as I allowed my mind to wander. Raquel's jade green eyes filled my thoughts. Her little face always seemed so sad and that haunted me. I wanted nothing more than to make her happy.

"And I, too," Cadmus agreed, reading my thoughts. "And we will. Once we get her back, she will be the happiest little girl in the world. I will make sure of it."

He bent to kiss my forehead and I clung to him, inhaling his strength. I would certainly need it on our quest. One final journey. It sounded so simple, like a last trip in an old car or a final visit to a store going out of business. But it wasn't the same.

Our journey would not be simple. I knew that already, even without using powers of prophecy. There would be pitfalls and obstacles and challenges that I couldn't even conceive of right now.

But I was stronger than I thought. I had proven that to myself time and time again. I was not weak...I was the Chosen One. And as the Chosen One, I knew that every journey since the beginning of time has always started with a single step. I sighed and swung my legs out of bed.

The End

For the dramatic conclusion to The Bloodstone Saga,
Please read *My Tattered Bonds*

AUTHOR'S NOTES

Was Camelot real?

No one knows. There is no historical evidence that King Arthur ever existed. He is mentioned in books written during the medieval times, but no factual evidence has ever been unearthed.

Regardless, there are many stories of this fabled hero that have been spun and passed down since the medieval times. The first account of his life was told by Geoffrey of Monmouth in his Latin work, *Historia Regum Brittaniae*. How much of this story was based in truth? Again, no one knows.

Some historians suggest that Arthur was actually one fictional character comprised of several different real-life heroes. Some suggest that he never existed at all. And still others believe that he did.

What no one disputes, however, is how widely loved and romanticized his story has become. Arthur and his Roundtable Knights have become the epitome of chivalry and honor—in fact, in the 19th century, a new code of ethics was established for gentlemen based upon Arthur's ideals. Chivalry and honor came in vogue again, creating a very genteel era.

I tried to keep the story of Camelot as true as possible to the already existing stories. It is said that Mordred was the downfall of the king, so I made him a villain. The story of Guinevere and Lancelot is legendary, so of course I had to make them Aphrodite and Ares. All of the knights that I used were said to have been actual Roundtable Knights.

Whether it was real or not... Camelot is something fun to think of. Who wouldn't want to believe that a place with perfect ideals and a chivalrous king, guarded by a legion of gentlemanly knights truly did exist? I certainly like to think it did, but then, I'm a romantic at heart.

And now, Book Four. Sigh. I love my characters so much that I am sad to bring this series to a close. But trust me, Book Four, *My Tattered Bonds*, will be epic. Harmonia and Cadmus' trials aren't over yet, but they are both strong and brave. I have no doubt that whatever they face, they will face it together. I hope you have enjoyed their story as much as I have enjoyed writing it. And now, I'm off to write the final book.

Thank you so much for reading my books. I appreciate each and every one of you so much.

ABOUT THE AUTHOR

Courtney Cole is a Young Adult novelist who would rather read and write than do just about anything else in the world.

She's had a fascination with Greek mythology for as long as she can remember, so of course she had to write about it in her first series.

Other books in The Bloodstone Saga: Every Last Kiss, Fated and My Tattered Bonds.

Other books by Courtney Cole: Guardian and Princess.

To learn more about Courtney, visit
www.courtneycolewrites.com

www.ingramcontent.com/pod-product-compliance
Lightning Source LLC
Chambersburg PA
CBHW050926120626
46552CB00001B/69